What's Next?

ISBN: 978-1-63950-067-3   [Paperback Edition]
      978-1-63950-068-0   [eBook Edition]

Printed and bound in The United States of America.

Writers Apex

Gateway Towards Success

8063 MADISON AVE #1252
Indianapolis, IN 46227
+13176596889
www.writersapex.com

What's Next?

A Short Biography of Bobby Bell

CHAPTER 1

Seven-year-old Anthony Gallagher held his brother Dennis's hand and looked up into his brother's blue eyes. "Denny, do you see that man over there by the tunnel?"

"You mean the guy wearing a suit in this Florida weather?"

"Don't you think it's kinda weird? I mean, it is hot outside, and he is the only one in a suit."

"Anthony, a lot a people wear suits, especially people who work in some kind of business, or maybe lawyers. Heck, even you sometimes wear a tie to school."

"Yeah, Denny, but he keeps looking over here."

* * *

Deplaning the 747 and exiting the tunnel from the aircraft into the arrival area, Russell had a feeling he was being stared at. Not so much him as the woman and children standing near him. Shaking his head and pondering his arrival, he couldn't help feeling, *Is it even possible to be a **little** paranoid? I guess no more than it is for a woman to be a little bit pregnant.* Eighteen months in a very inhospitable country, a place where he felt that his presence was not at all welcome. Plus it was miserably hot especially during daylight hours. It could get downright cold at night. He really couldn't help looking around. *Is that short dark man in a very expensive suit staring at me? No! He is definitely looking. Hell, he ain't looking, he is staring! I really need to talk to someone about this!* Taking a deep breath and letting it out slowly, he thought, *Life goes on.* Within minutes his wife will be in his arms and he will be with his kids.

Feeling as if he'd been in his dress blues for at least a week, Russell Gallagher couldn't believe he was actually home. Well, almost home. Tampa International Airport still looked the same. The air still had the smell of artificial air and a hundred bodies packed in the cabin of the 747. He looked at the small attractive woman with auburn hair standing with three children. *No, that can't be them. Those kids are way too big, and the auburn hair of the woman is wrong. When I left at this same gate eighteen months ago, my wife's hair came down to her shoulders. I do have three kids, but they couldn't have grown that much. That little red-headed girl with locks and the stuffed pink bunny is standing on her own. When I left, little Jackie was crawling and very... She actually would teeter until she found some something to hold onto—an end table, the coffee table, or the couch.*

"Rusty, Russ, over here." It was the woman. The boys were pulling away from her and running toward him.

A boy that stood almost up to his chest with dirty blond hair was running up to him. "Daddy! Here, over here." The boy behind him was a towhead, his complexion almost translucent it was so white, and had pale blue eyes. When Rusty asked, the doctor said no, he wasn't albino. His skin had pigmentation, but he had to be very careful in the sun. The doctor said he was healthy. He was a lot bigger than the Anthony he remembered when he left. The little girl with red locks just stood there hiding behind her mother with her stuffed bunny in her left hand and two fingers of her right hand in her nose with the thumb in her mouth.

The two boys were huddled around Russell with Anthony holding on to one pant leg, and Dennis holding his hand. Red-haired Jacquelyn with thumb still in her mouth held onto her mother's leg ever tighter and then put her arms up to be lifted into her mother's arms. Her eyes appeared the size of saucers, like a painting by Margaret Keane, and the same color as her mother's. He could never figure out the color of Naomi's eyes either. Hazel is what some people call them. She was just staring at her dad. Naomi looked back at Russ, motioning for him to follow her, trying to yell over the noise of the crowd. "What kind of bag are we looking for?"

Sweat ran down his nose and his shirt felt damp, sticking to his body. "Only one piece of luggage. The same olive drab duffle bag that I left with. I do have a few more things coming, but I put them in my hold baggage."

Putting Jackie down, Naomi said, "Jackie, you're a big girl. Can you walk beside Mommy for a while?"

Russ bent over to pick up Jackie. He didn't think her hazel eyes could get any bigger. Getting even closer to her mother, she said, "Mommy, I don't want that man to hold me."

"Jackie, that's your Daddy."

Squeezing into the small elevator, Russ looked over at his wife and pushed his hat back. "That's okay. Jacquelyn was just a little more than a twinkle when I left. We'll get to know one another."

Looking over at the maroon Chevy Caprice then at the kids and finally at Naomi, he said, "How's the car been running?"

Putting out his hand for the keys, he asked, "Do I get to drive? It has been a long time. The last thing I drove was a twenty-nine-passenger bus on the flight line.

"Naomi," he said, pointing to the small dark man in the very expensive suit. It was a blue suit, and he was wearing a pink shirt and red tie. "Is it me or have you noticed him staring at us?"

"Russ, you just got out of the Mideast. I'm sure he is not looking at us."

Climbing behind the steering wheel, looking over to the right and patting Russell on the shoulder, she said, "Russ, I know you like driving this car, but a few things have changed. First, I'm not living with the folks. I got a job as a legal aid in St. Pete. The drive from Sarasota to St. Pete was becoming a hassle, so we're renting a place on the north side of St. Pete. I got Denny and Anthony into the Catholic school. It's not that far from the house, plus I don't have to take Jackie to day care. The school actually has a day care."

Russell started shaking his hands as if they were on fire and blowing on his fingers. "Sorry about that, but my hands have been falling asleep lately, and my fingers get cold and then real hot like they're on fire. Sometimes it feels like I've got fire ants on my hands. I'm sure it's nothing. Probably a pinched nerve. St. Paul's?"

Naomi shook her head.

"I went there up to the eighth grade. I actually graduated out of the eighth grade. Actually the folks thought I'd be going on to Bishop Berry High School."

"Why didn't you go on to the Catholic high school? Too tough?"

"No, it wasn't too tough. It was girls. Kinda missed looking at them. Bishop Berry was an all-boys school back then.

Looking over at Russ with half a grin, she said, "I do hope it's only your hands that are numb."

There was quiet in the car. Even the kids seemed to be unusually quiet. Naomi spoke first. "I'd tell you to go over to the clinic, but if you could wait until you talk to your mom... She called yesterday and she wants you to call her as soon as you can. I think there might be something wrong with your dad."

Cresting the high point on the Gandy Bridge, he asked, "Did Mom say what was wrong?"

"She did say your dad was having some breathing problems and they have him on oxygen. She wanted to tell both of us about your dad."

He rubbed the back of his neck. "That oxygen must put a hell of a crimp on his smoking."

With her lips pressed tightly together, she said, "**Rusty** . . . that is not **even** funny."

Russ just couldn't believe how much Tampa Bay had changed. Coming off the Gandy Bridge, Naomi turned left on Ninth Street. Within minutes, she called to the backseat, "Denny, open the gate for Mommy! Denny... Dennis! Are you awake?"

"What color is that siding?"

"When we first rented it, I thought it was sand brown. The landlord informed me the shingle siding is actually what the landlord called desert brown."

Russ placed his hand on Naomi's knee. "Only in Florida could you get away with that color. I'd almost forgot about jalousie windows. This has got to be the only place in the world with jalousie windows." Pushing Naomi's skirt up above her knee, he said, "Naomi, I think I can handle the gate." Looking over at Naomi, he said, "I honestly don't know what I want first. Food or climbing into bed and sleeping for twelve hours."

In unison from the backseat, even little Jackie: "We want food."

"Naomi, have you been feeding these kids?"

"Yes, Russ, I do feed our children. Sometimes I don't eat, but my kids always get fed."

"I know they do."

"Rusty, you need to call your mom." The three kids were sitting at the kitchen table just staring. Anthony was holding a knife in one fist and a fork in the other. Russ had taken his shoes off and grabbed the phone. "Naomi, I can't remember their phone number."

After pulling out her address book and handing it to Russ, she walked into the small kitchen. "All right, guys. Daddy is calling his mother so please be quiet. We'll call for pizza."

At that there was an unusually hushed, "Yah."

"Naomi, what is that you have in your hand?"

"Oh! It's a cellular phone. I was told I needed it for work. The law firm is paying for it. I'm surprised you don't know what this is. I know some of the people over there in the desert were using them to call home."

With a raised eyebrow, she said, "Russ, you have to be the last person on the face of the earth that doesn't have a cell phone. Hell, homeless people have cell phones."

"Yeah, I've seen them, but they always seem too expensive. Some of the guys in my outfit were always running out of minutes."

Looking up at Russ who was coming out of the bedroom, she said, "Boy, that didn't take long. Did you get a chance to talk to your dad?"

"Yeah. He says it's as if he has a slight case of the flu. He doesn't know why the doc wants him to use that oxygen 24/7. I did ask if he has quit smoking. Says he knows better than to smoke near the oxygen tank. I told him we would come for a visit, but didn't know exactly when."

"My boss knows that I might need a little time off. So I have no problem. What about you?"

"I got thirty days. I might go and see my new boss, just to let my new bosses know what's going on. I suppose I could just tell my sponsor what's going on. I haven't met him yet, but we are already invited over for steaks. Says he'll burn them on the grill."

"Well, since you're off anyway, I'll go in tomorrow and let my boss know what's going on."

Rubbing his face and scratching his head, he pulled his wife toward him. "Dad seems to be doing pretty good for now. Mom says that it is hard for her to sleep. She hears that oxygen pumping and his breathing. She says it is worse than listening to his snoring. She got used to his labored breathing. It's when he stops that makes her sit up in bed."

Naomi sat on Russell's lap and leaned her head back. "So what are they doing about it?"

"Would you believe that Dad is on a list for a transplant? I didn't even know that they could do that."

"Yeah, that has become quite common."

"I know that there has been a lot of progress in heart transplants, but Dad's going to need a lung and heart transplant."

"Well, they are in Houston where they have some of the best in that field."

"Yeah, but they are doing it at the VA."

Just then the doorbell rang. Naomi pulled herself up off Russell's lap, "Okay, kids, pizza is here."

It seemed to Russell that the kids were on speed. They were literally bouncing off the walls. "Naomi! Where is the turn-off switch on these kids?"

Sounding like a marine drill instructor, Naomi shouted with a voice that was not quite a deep as a Marine's, at least the Marines Russ knew. "**All right!** Let's bring it down. Now all of you change into sleeping clothes, brush your teeth, and come out here when you're done so you can kiss me and Dad good night."

"Wow… you have that down. Remind me not to get on the wrong side of you?"

"Oh, Russ, I'm not mad, that is just how I do it. I've tried acting sweet. It doesn't work. For now this is the best I can do."

For about five minutes the house was completely quiet. Then it started just a little murmur, but the noise level was tolerable.

There was a little disturbance near the bathroom. "**Mom! Mom**, Anthony has been in the bathroom forever."

Her hands on her hips, she stood in the middle of the living room, "Anthony, are you sick? Do you need some medicine?"

They heard a voice muffled by the bathroom door and running water. "No, I'll be out as soon as I dry off."

Denny replied, "Yeah, but he is using all the hot water."

Jacquelyn came around the corner from the bedrooms with her hands up and walked hesitantly to her father. Looking up at him and raising her hands, she said, "Daddy?"

"Yes, Jackie, I'm your daddy." Reaching down and placing her on his lap, he said, "Are we friends now?"

Naomi stuck her head in one of the bedrooms. "Denny, Anthony, are you ready for bed?"

In unison: "Yes, ma'am."

"Well, come out here and say good night to your dad."

With Jackie in his lap, Russell looked up to see the boys. "Mom and I will tuck you guys in. Call after you say your prayers. Do you need me in there to make sure you pray? Remember to thank God for bringing me home safe."

Denny with his lips in a pout and Anthony with his hands hanging loosely in front of him answered, "Yes, ma'am."

Turning to Russell, she said, "I've got a little toddler's bed set up for Jackie in the room next to ours. Don't freak, but sometimes she'll climb into bed with me."

* * *

The night he had been thinking about and planning for over a year was not at all what he had expected, and he was evidently not the only one disappointed.

They slept turning their backs to one another, but for Russell sleep would not come. Putting his head close to Naomi's and listening, he could hear her steady deep breathing.

Pulling the sheets back and getting up, Russ tried to ease out of bed. As quietly as he could, he crept into the kitchen. Opening the refrigerator door, he was startled when he felt Naomi standing behind him, "I'm sorry. There's cold water in the fridge?" he asked.

"It feels as if I've got a mouthful of cotton. I guess that's better than sand? Listen, I am sorry."

Standing next to Russ, Naomi forced a smile. "Rusty, it has been a long time. It's okay."

Russ looked into the fridge. "I see we still have some iced tea. Is it sweet tea?"

"Yeah, I still can't get used to unsweetened tea. Since when did you quit smoking?"

"Evidently too soon, although this is a first for me. I could use a cigarette right now."

Putting ice in two glasses and pouring tea, he almost dropped the glasses. "I don't know what's wrong with me. One night about two months ago I ran out of smokes. I decided not to buy anymore. They just didn't taste right, so I quit."

"You said we were going to visit your folks, but you never said when?"

"I guess we need to make that trip to Houston soon. I was thinking we could leave after the weekend. Of course I can go alone."

"No way, mister. Plus your folks haven't seen the baby yet. You know your dad has cancer. We may never get another chance for the kids to be with him."

"Well, he didn't act like he needed to see us right away. Plus we probably should wait until we find out when he's going into surgery."

"The boys will be on Easter vacation in a week. Maybe we could plan the trip for during Easter vacation."

"I'll call Mom tomorrow and tell her our plans."

Grabbing Russell's hand, she said, "Let's go back to bed. Don't worry, just hold me. You know I did miss you."

The first rays of light were coming through the window. Russ pulled Naomi close to him. "Now I think I could use that cigarette."

Pushing her hair out of her eyes, she asked, "What time is it?" Squinting at the clock radio on the dresser, she exclaimed, "Oh! Shit, we got to get the boys ready for school."

Jackie was the first to show up in the kitchen. "Mommy, yum, yum.

"There's cerul up there, Daddy," Jackie said, pointing to the cupboard.

Turning to Russell, Naomi added, "The bowls are in the cupboard next to the pantry."

Denny came out of the bedroom, his hair needing combing and his shoelaces tied. Anthony sat at the table in front of his cereal. Russell noticed something wrong with his shirt. He had a clip-on tie and a shirt with a collar, but he had only buttoned the top two buttons. Jackie still had her pink pajamas with pictures of blue bunnies. Without even turning, Naomi picked her up and placed her in the high chair.

Heading for the bathroom, Naomi turned back and stopped, "Russ, do you think you could find your old elementary school?"

"Denny, Anthony, are you boys ready?"

Wearing a blue collared shirt with clip-on tie, his shirttail hanging outside his gray slacks, Anthony headed for the car with Russ trailing. With eyebrows raised, Russ asked, "Okay, Anthony, where is your brother?"

"He had to go to the bafroom."

After opening the car doors and directing Anthony to the backseat, Russ climbed behind the steering wheel and turned to say, "Buckle up now."

Leaning over the front seat, Anthony tapped his father on the shoulder. "Daddy, Daddy, I dreameded about you when you were away."

"I thought I told you to buckle up?"

"I will, Daddy, when Denny gets here. Did you hear me, Daddy. I dreamded about you when you were in the war."

Looking back at his son, Russ said, "Well, you know I dreamed about you too."

"Was you scared when the road exploded in front of you and blew up? What was that smell? My eyes burned. It was so bright, and my nose was burning. It was burning so bad that my eyes hurt and I was crying. You were really brave, Dad."

"Anthony, did your mom tell you about that explosion?"

He thought about the night he ran to the bunker. *I don't remember writing about that night. I know because I didn't want to worry Naomi. There are weird things going on with my body. I haven't been sleeping well, and I **am** forgetting things. Maybe I did write about it?*

"Did your mom tell you about that?" Russ said just as Denny showed up.

"Sorry, Dad, but I didn't think I could hold it."

"School still start at eight?"

"Yes, sir, but we meet in church and then walk to school with the class," Denny replied.

"Well, we still have time."

Russell stopped at the curb in front of the church and watched his boys run up the steps to the double doors of the church. Somewhere in the back of his mind he was remembering lugging his newly covered textbooks up those steps. He could see in his mind's eye how he used to get up early to serve mass. *Things have certainly changed*, he thought as he looked back at the two-story red brick building that was his school. He didn't ask his wife if they still separated the boys and the girls, with the boys on one side of the building and the girls on the other.

There was a small woman walking up the sidewalk toward the church. She had a pale blue skirt, white blouse, and what looked like a blue scarf. She turned to look at him and he could see the large rosaries at her waist and the cross around her neck.

Still what Anthony told him this morning was gnawing at his mind. *I still have all the letters Naomi sent me. They are in a cigar box I kept in my duffel bag, now at the bottom of my dresser drawer. I need to look through them to see if she mentions that night so long ago in another world. Yet it was only twelve months ago.*

Russ called the boys back to the car. Denny looked out of breath, "What's the matter, Dad?"

Pointing to the woman in the pale blue dress, Russ asked, "Is that one of your teachers?"

Both boys turned to look. Anthony answered, "No, I think she is a nun. My teacher is not a nun."

Denny chimed in, "Mine neither."

CHAPTER 2

Putting his large callused hands up to his eyes and squinting against the glare from the sun through a dirt-crusted windshield, Melvin Wright watched as he opened the door of the van and beer cans tumbled out. He turned his large frame from behind the steering wheel and swung his booted feet and long legs out of the door. Putting his arms around his bare chest with a shiver against the cold, he unzipped the fly of his stained khaki pants and urinated. Pulling his fly up and reaching back in the van, he felt around for the dash, grabbing a crumpled cigarette pack and finding one bent cigarette. He found his cigarette lighter stuck in the crease of the front seat cushion. Unsuccessfully he tried to light the cigarette. After several tries, he finally put the tip of his finger over the hole in the cigarette, drawing in the sweet smoke. With a coughing spasm, he stuck his head in the van and looked back. Taking a breath after the coughing stopped, he saw Darlene lying in the empty cargo area in a fetal position with both hands holding her stomach. She was moaning. Her moans were soft, so he could barely hear them. If it weren't for the convulsive-like shaking, he would not have known she had been moaning. Beside Darlene was an empty syringe. She still had a rubberlike tube around her arm just above her elbow.

Banging on the side of the cargo van, Melvin yelled. "Darlene! Darlene, get up, we have to move." Moving away from the van, he felt his well-worn boots sink in the mud. He also felt the mud seeping up around his toes. He shouted to the back of the van. "Darlene, did Larry call?"

She coughed up phlegm and spat before she spoke. "Melvin, where are we?"

"I'm not sure. There are a lots of trees, shrubs, and it looks like a cypress next to a river. It sure don't smell like roses here, more like a backed-up sewer. I asked if you got any calls on that cell phone."

"It's not working."

"What do you mean it's not working?"

"Oh, a message pops up saying I need to make a payment."

"Ah, shit."

Cupping his hands and holding them above his eyes, he said, "I think I see a shack on stilts. Looks like the shack is sitting right over the water."

Just then there was a screech and the flutter of wings. Darlene screamed. "What was that?"

Looking up, Melvin saw a large white bird with black tipped wings. Reaching into the van, he grabbed the tee shirt that was rolled up in a ball under the front seat, sniffed the shirt, and pulled it over his head. "I think that was a crane." Still watching the crane as it climbed into the air, he saw several white ibis stalking through the grass near the shoreline of the river in their jerky-leggy way, looking, Melvin assumed, for bugs and worms.

Grabbing a roll of toilet paper, Darlene pushed the doors at the rear of the van open, forcing unkempt mousy brown hair away from her eyes. Running for one of the higher growing shrubs, she looked over at Melvin with a look of pain. "Melvin, I don't feel so good. You think you might be able to get me some paregoric?"

"Darlene, I don't know where we are. I remember passing the sign for Slidell, and then Tammany Parish."

Coughing and clearing more phlegm from her throat, she said, "You think maybe you could get me some Scat?"

"Baby, like I said, I don't know where **here** is, and even if I did, we don't have any money."

Coming out from behind the shrub, she pulled her jeans up, making an effort to straighten her blue tank top, "Baby, you always know how to take care of me. You have any beer left? It might just settle my stomach."

Climbing behind the wheel and motioning for Darlene to get in the van, he said, "We need to get out of this damn swamp."

Three tries and the engine finally turned over. Stepping on the gas did nothing but make the back wheels spin, digging the van deeper in the mud. "Foregut me." Looking over at Darlene, he said, "Get over here behind the wheel. I'll push. Just wait until I tell you, and then step on the gas. Not hard but easy."

The wheels still spinning, he barked, "Darlene, put it in reverse, then in drive." Now the wheels were digging in in both directions.

Sticking her head out of the window, she shouted, "Now, what?"

"Grab our packs. Let's go over to that shack. I don't think there's anyone there."

He heard a gurgle as Darlene tried to clear her throat. "Then what are we going to do?"

"Maybe we can find a shovel or some rocks or maybe a two-by-four. Something to use to get us out of the mud." Melvin did find an army-issue pick and shovel in the shack.

* * *

The sun was high in the sky by the time they got the van free of the mud. Back in the shack, over the water, he remembered seeing several cans on a shelf, mostly beans. Digging his Swiss Army knife out of his packet and using the can opener attachment, he opened a can of beans. He and Darlene took turns putting the can to their lips, sucking the beans out of the can.

Digging into Darlene's large handbag, Melvin found a hairbrush and managed to get his black, gray-specked hair back with the use of a scrunchy he found in Darlene's handbag and put his hair in his usual ponytail.

* * *

Looking out the doorway and back at Melvin, Darlene said, "It's hot. Do you think that river water is cold? Ya know, maybe we could clean up a little? I'd feel a little better."

With a lot of oohs and aahss, they managed to splash enough river water on their naked bodies and face to get most of the grime off, splashing under their arms to lessen some of the smell.

Melvin sat down in the river water, letting the water come up to his chin. "Come over here, Darlene. This was your idea." It was then that Melvin stood up, "Hey baby, did you hear that?"

"Hear what?"

"I thought I heard a splash."

"That was you."

"Oh! Funk! Move! Get out of the water."

"What is it?"

Melvin pointed to the shoreline. "Look over there. About fifty feet down there on the shoreline."

Cuffing her hand above her eyes, Darlene said, "All I see is an old log down there."

"Darlene, that ain't no log. That is a 'gator, and I think we woke him up from his nap." Grabbing Darlene by the back of her neck, he whispered, "Move, Darlene. I think he's pissed."

Without actually running, they both made it to the shack, away from what looked to Melvin like a 'gator that had to be a least twenty feet long.

Taking a deep breath and digging jeans out of his backpack, Melvin said, "Put some clothes on, Darlene. Let us try and find a town."

* * *

Backing up on the muddy track, the van turned carefully and moved slowly under Spanish moss-laden oak trees. It started sliding momentarily, the wheels finally grabbing traction as they entered a two-lane asphalt road.

Reaching for the crumbled cigarette pack and feeling inside the crumbled pack, Melvin let out a sigh of frustration. Glancing at Darlene, he spoke: "I think I remember seeing a sign for Pearl River. I don't know whether it was just the name of a river or a town, but if there are enough people I'm sure we can score something."

"Like some Scat?"

With sarcasm, he said, "Darlene, would you please knock it off about your medicine."

"I'm sorry, Melvin. I am feeling a little better."

Sticking his hands first in his front pockets, then in his rear pockets, in his threadbare shirt pocket, and finally tearing through his canvas wallet, he found a small piece of paper. "I need to call Larry. He said he'd call me. But our phone don't work! He has probably been trying to reach us."

"How you gonna get hold of this guy? I mean, you never been here before. Have you?"

"No, I don't think so, but I do have this guy Larry's phone number," he said, pointing to the small piece of paper.

"Good thing I saved his number. I didn't worry 'cause he was supposed to call us."

"Melvin, when I miss my medicine I get a bad stomachache. Sometimes I have diarrhea so bad that I don't think I'll ever get off the toilet."

Putting his hand up as if to stop her from talking, he said, "I know, baby, I'll get something for you. Now just shut up about your bellyache."

"Melvin, this time is worse than ever. It even hurts when I try to pee. It looks like I'm peeing Coca cola."

"Okay. You want me to find you a doctor. You know we can check into the emergency room. They got to take you."

"I'll be quiet." With a groan and a sigh, she said, "If we go to the hospital, they will put me in rehab, or worse."

"Hey, rehab's not that bad. The food is not all that good, but they do feed you."

They drove through deep ditches on both sides of the black asphalt highway, shrubs growing on the sides of the deep ditches and oak trees with Spanish moss hanging down almost to the road, looking like an archway. Looking down at the speedometer, Melvin noticed the engine light flashing low fuel, suddenly hearing what sounded like a fart. He looked over at Darlene. She raised her shoulders, mouthing the words. All of a sudden they both heard a clunk, followed by a clank. The van shivered. Then came the sound of corn popping. The van threatened to die. Then it did die. He tried to restart the engine, only to hear several clicks. Melvin managed to coast over as far as he can without sliding into the ditch.

In the haze of the sun, humidity, and heat, Melvin made out what looked like old-fashioned gas pumps. Motioning for Darlene to slide out of the van through the driver's side, he said, "Darlene, I see a gas station up the road. Let's get us some gas, and maybe just a little cash."

Following Melvin out of the van, she said, "Melvin, how we gonna do that?"

Walking closer to the gas pumps, looking first to the right and then to the left, he saw a sign above what looked like a little convenience store. "Darlene, see that sign. I can't read it, can you?"

"Yeah, Melvin."

"Well, baby, what does it say?"

With a little giggle, she answered, "It says sandwiches, beer, and bait."

"Well, Darlene, I sure would like a nice cold beer."

"But, Melvin, we ain't got no money."

Opening his eyes wide, putting his hands on his cheeks, with irony, he said, "Darlene, you know what to do. You just bat your eyes and I'll borrow us a little cash, and maybe get some gas for the van."

The little bait shack and gas station looked to be about maybe a quarter mile, but wiping sweat off his brow, Melvin thought it might as well be a hundred miles. The gravel on the side of the road was working its way into the holes in the bottom of his boots. Darlene was walking slower and slower until Melvin finally stopped and looked back at her. "Darlene, you want to get somthen for that pain in your belly?"

Taking a deep breath, she bent over and put her hands on her knees. "Yes, Melvin. Don't be mad. Just give me a sec to catch my breath."

"Okay, Darlene." Pointing to a large Spanish moss-covered oak tree closest to the road, a few feet away from the drainage ditch, he said, "See that oak tree?"

Darlene looked down the road and squinted against the glare of the sun. "Melvin…," she cleared her throat. "There are a lot of trees."

"Well, Darlene," he said with sarcasm, "it's the big one on this side of the ditch." Walking over to the tree and sitting cross-legged, Melvin proceeded to pull off his left boot, rubbing his toes and shaking a pebble out of the boot. He pulled his gray sock up and put the boot back on. "Five minutes. We got to get out of the sun."

Squatting against the tree, sniffling, she looked up at Melvin. "Thank you, Melvin. Just give me a few minutes."

Later she said, "Melvin, don't you find it weird that we haven't seen any traffic on this road? Where are we anyway? I don't see no signs."

"Kinda. No, I haven't, and I have no idea."

"What?" she said, trying to get to her feet and looking around.

"No, Darlene, I ain't seen no traffic, and I haven't even seen a mile marker. Yes, it is kinda weird. I wonder if there's gonna be anyone in that bait shop, but if you look down toward the river, there a few small cabins. Must be that fishing camp we saw on the sign a ways back."

Almost out of breath, Darlene walked up to the door, which may have been at one time painted white, but appeared to be chipped dull yellow. Breathing heavily, she asked, "What now, Melvin?"

He let out a long sigh. "You go in first. I'll just go around back. I need to take a leak."

"What am I supposed to do?"

"You know what to do. Looks like there's only one person in there. Give him a sad story. You know how your car broke down and how you think you got the flu or somthen. Tell him you need gas for the car."

Fishing lures were displayed on a peg board behind a counter with a cash register in the middle. At the end of the counter near a wall next to a tank with live bait were fishing rods and poles with nets on the end. There was a tall skinny boy with his back turned to Darlene. With her hands on the counter, she said, "Excuse me, sir. Excuse me."

Darlene looked up at the man and found herself looking at the biggest Adam's apple she had ever seen, it was almost obscene, like a very large tumor.

Looking down directly into her eyes, he said, "Cher, how can I help you?"

No matter how pitiful she tried to sound, the tall skinny man with the biggest Adam's apple she ever saw and hair like yellow straw sticking out of a John Deer ball cap would not give an inch. "Cher, I can let ya use the phone, but I be the only one here. Can't leave. You want to buy something?"

As the skinny man turned back to the shelf, Melvin casually walked in. He slid behind the counter and with his Swiss Army knife, the large blade out, he grabbed the man's head, pushed it forward and down, and drew the blade just over his large Adam's apple.

Banging on the register until the drawer finally opened, Melvin looked in the drawer and looked over at Darlene, "Awe, funk, I don't even think there's fifty bucks here."

Darlene just stood staring at the boy—rather, man—sliding down to the floor. "Melvin, did you have to do that?"

"What? I discovered that if you put the head down the neck, it won't spirt blood."

"No, Melvin. Did you have to kill him?"

"Well, he said nobody else was here," Melvin said, grabbing a couple packs of cigarettes and handing the bills he just pulled out of the register to Darlene. "I'll get us one of them gas cans. Maybe we can get enough gas to get down the road. Now there is no one to tell nobody what we look like."

Walking back toward their van, Darlene called, "Wait up. Why couldn't I wait at the store for you? You know I'm sick."

"You want to be there when somebody does show up? I should have grabbed a cold six-pack. Trouble bein' if someone did happen to drive by and saw be luggen a six-pack, they just might get a little suspicious."

"Now you can go back to that bait shack if you want, but what if one of them fishermen decides he needs more bait. Well, do you want to go back and wait?"

Whining like a child that has been punished, she said, "Noo."

After several tries, Melvin got the van started. "Well, Darlene you gonna stand out there or get in the van."

"I'm getting in."

Driving by the bait shack, Melvin shook Darlene. "Look over there." There were two cars with flashing blue and red lights attached to a bar on the roof of their cars and state decals on the doors. "I was kinda hopen we could fill up the tank, maybe get a six-pack. A cold beer would be great."

* * *

They were finally on an interstate highway. "Darlene! Darlene, wake up!"

"What is it, Melvin?"

"How much money you got?"

"I got whatever you gave me."

Sighing, "Well, Darlene, how much did I give you?"

"Oh…" Digging into her handbag, she said, "Let me count it." Holding the bills and counting one at a time, she answered, "It looks like about sixty-three dollars."

"About? Well, is it sixty-three dollars or not?"

Counting again, she said, "Yeah, Melvin. It's sixty-three dollars."

Putting both hands on the wheel, he looked toward the right and then leaned closer to the windshield. "I see a sign saying there was food and gas at the next exit. I hope that exit ain't too far."

"Melvin," she said with that irritating nasal sound. "Melvin, you past the exit."

"Awe, shit." Melvin yanked the steering wheel to the right, the wheels spinning in the loose sand and scattering gravel on the side of the road. He turned sharply, realizing he was turning in the opposite directions as the blaring of horns reminded him that he was heading the wrong way. He did notice several people with their middle finger up. He didn't have to be a lip reader to understand some of what the people were saying.

Darlene held on to the handhold above the passenger-side window. "Melvin… I don't want to die."

The van teetered in a precarious position, finally righting. "Stop your whining. We made it."

Walking into the gas station convenience store, he checked out the counter and then looked around the store. There had to be at least a dozen people wandering the aisles or waiting for a sandwich at the deli counter at the back of the store. He walked up to the clerk and handed him fifty dollars. Looking up at the freckled red-headed clerk, he said, "I'm at pump three. Not sure how much it will take."

After pumping forty dollars worth in the tank, he stuck his head out the window and said, "I didn't fill it but I think we got enough gas to get to the next town."

Pushing her hair back away from her eyes and licking her lips, she asked, "Do we have enough left over for my medicine?"

He glanced at Darlene, looking into eyes sunken so deeply that all he could see were two deep dark holes. Her cough had become almost rhythmic that she was holding a dirty rag up to her running nose, "Darlene, you couldn't even get a taste for ten dollars, but we just might be able to get a cold six-pack. Once we get to town I'll be better able to figure out how we can get some money."

"Melvin, if you let me go inside, I'm sure I can find some man that will help us out."

"No, Darlene. We don't need to draw attention to ourselves. Besides I don't like to see you doin' that no more."

"You just don't think I look good enough anymore."

"Just hang in there. Once we get to some town I'll give Larry a call. Then he'll send us enough money to get what we need."

CHAPTER 3

Russell came up behind Naomi as she put a wrapped sandwich and an apple in a baggy and then in a brown paper lunch bag. "Just where do you think you're going?"

Turning her head so that Russ can give her a peck on the cheek, she said, "I thought I better get it over with. You know Jack has been pretty good with me. He's put up with me taking off when I had to take one of the kids to the doctor. I think I owe it to him to give a two-week notice."

"Believe me, I'd love to have you home," he said, pulling one chair out from under the kitchen table and motioning for Naomi to sit. Pulling another chair out and setting it next to her, he said, "Naomi, we need to talk."

She sat on the edge of the chair like she was about to run a race. "Russ, we'll have plenty of time to talk, but I really don't want to be late. I'm going to be asking for a couple weeks off. Plus I'll put in my notice."

Taking a deep breath then letting it out, he said, "This will only take a minute. What I tried to tell you last night is that you can quit. That's fine with me. But if you'd like to keep your job for a while, that's fine too."

Sounding a little frustrated and pursing her lips, she answered, "Listen, mister, when you joined the air force we agreed that we as a family would go wherever you went if we could. You know when the orders say accompanied, I intend to be the one that does the accompanying."

"Well, I thought maybe I could commute."

Looking up and raising her eyebrows, she said, "Okay. What's up?"

"I tried to tell you that my new assignment is right across the bay. I've already been communicating with my sponsor. Rumor has it that I'll probably be the new NCOIC of base operations."

Naomi jumped up and put her arms around his neck.

"Now, lady, if you really like that job of yours you better get. Don't forget to ask for two weeks around Easter."

"Since I didn't go in yesterday I'm not sure what time I'll get off. Would you drop me off at work and take the kids to school? Oh yeah, you'll need to pick them up. I'll call you when I'm ready for a ride. Oh, if you want you don't need to put Jackie in day care. That's if you think you're up to taking care of a three-year-old."

With a start, Russ looked up, "Where did Anthony go?"

Pointing to the driveway, she said, "That's him. Looks like he is putting the car seat in."

Russ gently moved Anthony out of the way. Exasperated after several tries at getting the car seat fastened in the backseat, Dennis finally came and with little effort fastened the seat in the middle of the backseat. "Okay, wise guy, slide in the backseat. We'll drop you guys off first."

"I thought Mom wanted to go in to work first?"

Looking over at Naomi then the boys, he said, "Naomi, what time do you need to be at work?"

"Jack likes his office staff in by nine. The partners stagger in whenever."

"Are you one of the partners?"

Raising her eyes, she said, "No, Russell, I am not a partner. I deal with some people mainly people that are filing bankruptcy The rest of the time I file records and do some typing."

"Okay. We take the kids in first. After all you work downtown, and if I'm not mistaken their school is less than ten minutes from here."

Tapping Anthony on the shoulder, he said, "What are you waiting for?" He pointed to the backseat. "Okay, you guys climb in the back with your sister."

* * *

Naomi placing her hand on Russ' knee. "What would you say to tuna casserole for supper? If you haven't changed too much, I seem to remember that you preferred not eating meat on Fridays."

"Sounds great. You doin' a casserole or salad?"

"I was thinking of the casserole."

"The tuna helper out of the box?"

"No. Tuna helper wouldn't even satisfy Jackie. Your kids are no pickers when it comes to eating. I had a girlfriend over for dinner, and when she saw how much they ate, she said she would rather clothe them than feed them any day."

At the table watching his kids eat, Russ jumped up after the last plate and the casserole dish were empty and cleared the table.

"Russell, I would have cleaned the table. Just relax. Your time will come."

"I was afraid they would eat the plates. Did you see how fast I moved my hands?"

Sitting at the table with his hands neatly folded and looking up at his dad, Denny said, "Can we get up now?

Looking at the kids, Naomi said with just a little wonder in her voice, "Since when do you wait for permission to leave the table? I'm not complaining. As a matter of fact, I would like to see that all the time."

With his elbows on the table and leaning on his hands, Anthony remarked, "Just waiting for Dad to tell us when we're taking our trip."

Still in her high chair, Jackie wiped her face with the back of her hand and looked first at her brothers then at her dad.

"Well, Anthony, you're right, but you know we are taking a trip to visit your grandparents. I just wanted to tell you that we will be here for Sunday mass, but early Monday we are taking off for Houston."

With a burp, Anthony looked at his mom and then his dad, "We really won't be leaving till Tuesday."

Turning to face her second son and wiping her hands on a dish towel, Naomi said, "Anthony! Why would you say that?"

"'Cause Daddy will need to get some medicine on Monday."

"Why would you say that?" Russell replied.

"'Cause you will, but we'll still get to go on Tuesday."

Taking charge, Naomi once again sounded like a drill sergeant. "Okay, boys. You can watch television for a little while." She reached down for Jackie. "And you, young lady, need a bath."

With her hands up above her head and waiting to be picked up, Jackie said, "Me watch tee bee too."

Naomi pulled at Jackie's little undershirt off. "Well, young lady, we'll see."

Plopping down in the big overstuffed recliner and looking over at the boys, who if they were any closer would literally have their noses glued to the screen, Russ said, "Slide back about five feet. By the way, Anthony, what did you mean we would have to wait for me to get my medicine?"

Denny broke in, "Well, Daddy, if Anthony says we got to wait for you to get your medicine, we will have to wait until you get your medicine."

"The only medicine I have ever taken was an aspirin."

The boys fell asleep in front of the TV. Jackie was just about asleep when Naomi lifted her out of the tub.

Pulling the sheets back, Russell looked over at Naomi. "I don't know why I'm so keyed up. I mean I spent over a year in the desert. If anything this trip should be like a walk in the park."

Climbing into the bed and scooting up against Russell, she remarked, "Aw… Your feet are cold. It really isn't cold at all. It has been up in the 80s all day. It ain't that much lower now."

"Sorry, but that's been happening a lot lately. When I get a few minutes, I'm going to have to see a doctor 'bout that. I never had a problem with circulation before."

"You know, Russ, that's the reason I married you." Russell turned toward her with raised eyebrows. "You know I was looking for a warm body to snuggle up against."

"I do hope you found other attributes other than a warm body."

"Oh, yeah. Which reminds me. Did you and your dad have a good relationship?"

"Not really. Oh my dad wasn't abusive or anything. I just don't think he liked me very much."

"Didn't you guys ever do things together? You know, like play catch or go fishing together. Did he ever take you to a ball game, like you do with the boys? Remember you took Denny and Anthony to watch the Yankees."

"I think we may have gone to a ball game. But if we did it was rare."

"Me and my dad were never close. I tried. I was ten when he retired from the army. You know what I think is worse than abuse? I think being ignored is worse. I always got the impression that he didn't like me. The only reason I agreed to this trip is because of Mom."

* * *

Throwing the sheets back, Russ pushed himself up, feeling some stiffness in his left shoulder. He thought he probably slept on it wrong. He swung around with more than a little more effort than he expected, finally sitting on the side of the bed. Pain shot up his legs as he tried to stand. He couldn't close his hands, which looked like balloons. He tried again to stand but fell back down on the side of the bed. He called out, "Naomi! Naomi, where are you?"

He heard a muffled sound from behind the closed bathroom door. "Russ, I'll be right out, just give me a minute." He could hear the sound of the toilet flushing, then a squeak as the bathroom door opened. Without looking up, he heard her say, "Russ, remind me to call someone when we get back to fix that door..." Looking at her husband sitting on the edge of the bed, she asked, "What in the world happened to you?"

"I don't know, but I can't stand or close my hands."

Bending down and attempting to help Russ to his feet, she asked, "Can you try to stand?"

"Naomi, there is no way you are going to be able to lift me."

"The number for the base clinic is by the phone in the living room."

While waiting, Russell did manage to clumsily limp into the bathroom.

With just a little panic in her voice, Naomi said, "Russ, I called the Air Force Hospital. They told me to take you to the E.R. here in St. Pete. They said if you can't walk I was to call an ambulance."

"I think I can make it to the car. What about the kids?"

"The car seat is still in the car."

Naomi walked into the boys' room and her eyes opened wide as she saw the boys were dressed, and Denny had his sister in his room trying to help her get dressed. "What's going on, boys?"

"Anthony woke me up and told me we was goin' to the hospital with you and Dad."

"Thank you so much for getting the baby ready. We have to take Dad to the emergency room. Evidently they don't believe in emergencies over at the air base." With a sigh Naomi walked back into her bedroom, noticing that Russ was not there. "Russ, are you here?"

"Yeah, Naomi. I'm in the bathroom. Be out in a sec."

Walking over to the bathroom door, sticking her head in the door then holding her nose, she said, "Woo! That ain't roses. Are you able to walk now?"

"Yeah. It's weird. My ankle hurts, but not really that bad. It's like my feet are numb, but the pain is almost tolerable. It's just that I don't have control. I'm unsteady." Pulling his trousers up, he attempted to pull his fly up, without much luck. "Look at my hands. You ever take one of those rubber gloves and blow it up like a balloon? Well?" Holding his hand up in front of Naomi, he said, "I wonder if I could make a balloon animal out of my hands."

"You are not funny, mister. Now come over here, if you can, and let me pull the zipper of your fly up."

* * *

After a shot of some sort of steroid, Russ was sent home to rest with a Zithromax Z-Pak. As for a diagnosis, the medics could not come up with anything other than influenza of the joints and advice for him to promise he would contact his personal physician.

Within a half hour the swelling in his hands had gone down and he was able to close his fist. Everyone was thrilled when Russ talked Naomi into stopping in at the local IHOP. Eggs, sausage, hash browns, and pancakes for the boys; little pancakes in the shape of Mickey Mouse for Jacquelyn; eggs benedict for Naomi; and chicken fingers and waffles for Russ.

After a walk around Mirror Lake, with Jackie chasing the ducks, the family went back to the house. Russ reassured everyone that he was feeling fine and they would start their trip to Houston in the morning.

By 5:30 in the evening, Jackie was holding her tummy and crying. Russ called her over to him and told her to sit in his lap. "Naomi, we got any Sprite in the fridge?"

"Yeah."

"Pour a small glass and let it sit for a few minutes. As soon as it gets to room temperature, bring it to me."

Russ placed the glass near Jackie's lips, "Now Jackie, Daddy wants you to drink this."

With her lips tight and after little cajoling, she finally opened her mouth and held the glass, first sipping then drinking the little bit of Sprite in one gulp. Within seconds Jackie let out a burp and a little fart. "Daddy, I feel better now."

That night the kids appeared to be bouncing off the walls. Russ could swear he could see the energy in the room. By nine the silence was overwhelming. Watching some sitcom that he wasn't really paying attention to, he turned to his wife. "Now I'm keyed up."

Naomi got up and headed for the bedroom. "Russell, I think I can help you. Come on. Get yourself a nice hot shower and come to bed."

CHAPTER 4

Pulling next to one of two gas pumps in front of a convenience store, Melvin turned to Darlene. "Well, baby, you know what to do."

Feeling phlegm in the back of her throat, Darlene manage to hack it up and spit out the window. Wiping her mouth, she said, "Melvin, I don't like doing that. I'm cramping real bad. Do you think they'll let me use the toilet in there?"

"Darlene, that is gross."

"I know, that's why I don't like doing that."

"Not that, but spitting out the window is gross. I think it's some kinda health law where they have a public restroom, especially where they sell food."

Wiping her mouth and opening the door, she answered, "Oh."

"While you're at it, wipe off the side of the door too."

As she opened the door to the little convenience store, the bell hooked to the top of the door rang. Darlene looked up with a start. As she looked over at the counter, she felt her heart stop when she saw two policemen leaning against the counter, sipping a steaming beverage out of a paper cup. The clerk looked up and the policemen—the blond one with a buzz cut, the other very tall with dark hair—turned to stare at her. With a hard swallow, she said, "Excuse me. I think we're lost."

Just as the police officer started to answer, Melvin walked in, "Sorry, did I interrupt something?"

Digging into a large ice chest, Melvin pulled out a beer. "That road gets my throat mighty parched."

The taller of the two policemen spoke up. "You're not thinken of drinking that while you're driving, are you?"

"No, sir. We were planning of camping when we got through town."

"Well, this ain't much of a town." Looking over at the clerk, he said, "There's a nice little campsite about eleven miles out of town. That is if you are heading north. Don't get many people camping this time of year. Now next month the campers will be coming in force."

"Well, thanks. Me and the missus will be headen for the camp grounds." Looking over at the clerk, a small framed teenager with acne scars on his face, he said, "You wouldn't happen to have a phone I could use?"

The smaller blond police officer turned and with raised eyebrows said, "Sorry, I'm Deputy Wilson." Pointing to the taller one, he said, "This here is Deputy Samson. Most folks today carry cell phones. I'm sure Daryl can let you use the phone if it's a local call."

"Got one, but the carrier would like payment before they turn it on. No, sir, it's not local. It's to my employer, but it is a 1-800 number."

Pointing to the back of the store behind the display counters, the clerk said, "Ya know, I got cell phones here that only cost ten bucks."

Darlene just stared at Melvin. Melvin looked at the deputies and then at Daryl. "Not this time but maybe later. That's kinda why I need to call my boss. We had a little car trouble and I need to get an advance on my pay."

As Melvin headed back toward the payphone, the tall deputy spoke up. "If I ever called the lieutenant to tell him I needed an advance, after he finished laughing he'd tell me to walk."

Motioning for Darlene to come closer, the tall cop asked, "You feeling all right lady?"

Trying to keep from looking in the deputy's eyes, Darlene answered, "Yeah, well no. I think I might have the stomach flu. Maybe I just ate something that isn't agreeing with me."

The clerk pointed to the back of the store. "There's a public restroom back there."

Walking back toward the restrooms, Darlene called back to Melvin. "Mel, I'll wait out in the van."

Holding his hand over the mouthpiece of the telephone, he answered, "Okay, Darlene."

"Darlene, is that your name? Darlene?" Daryl asked.

"Yeah, I mean yes."

Coming out of the restroom, she looked up, not seeing Melvin.

The clerk pointed to the door. "The coffee's free. Take a cup with you." Once back in the van, within minutes Darlene was asleep.

Melvin had to shake Darlene to wake her. "I got hold of Larry. He said that we can pick up two grand at eight tomorrow morning. Said that he'll wire it to us. Will be able to pick the money up at any Super Walmart."

Sitting up and leaning forward, Darlene started hacking until she was able to clear the phlegm from her throat. She opened the door and spat. Taking a stained handkerchief from her purse, she wiped her lips and turned to Melvin. "I didn't get any of that nastiness in your van."

"You still feeling bad? I notice you are sweating. It really ain't that hot. Matter a fact, it's getting downright cold out here."

Darlene started to shake, unable to keep her hands steady. "Melvin, you got any money left? Maybe enough to get me a little taste."

"Whatever money we got is in your purse, but I don't think you'll find any."

"Where did you get the money to pay for the beer?"

"I kept five out just for something like that."

"You can afford a beer, but I can't get what I need?"

"It's a good thing I did. It would have sure made those cops suspicious if I came in there without getting somthen'.

"Which way is north?" he said, banging his hands on the steering wheel. "And where the hell is a Walmart?"

Pulling into a gas station that was lit up like an airport runway, Melvin said, "Darlene, go in there and find out where the closest Walmart is."

Sweat covering her brow, Darlene opened the passenger-side door and climbed up into the seat. "The lady behind the counter said the closest Walmart is back toward Slidell."

"Did you ask about a Western Union?"

"No. You didn't tell me to."

After making several stops for Darlene, they tried to stop at the roadside rest areas, pulling off onto the shoulder and shielding Darlene with the van door. A trip that should have taken less than an hour took them almost two hours. They were finally at a 24-hour Walmart.

"Why are you parking so far from the doors?"

"Well, if I know Walmart, there a' probably cameras in their parking lot. I don't really think we can pick up our money until morning."

The sun was shining through the van window. After several trips to the restroom inside the Walmart, Darlene shook Melvin. "Is it time yet to pick up our money?"

Stretching and popping the door open, he looked at his watch. "It's not quite time, but maybe somebody will be there to check on the MoneyGram?"

Coming out of the restroom, Darlene noticed that Melvin was sleeping on the bench right inside the entrance. Darlene shook him. "Melvin, I think the bank is open."

A skinny, blond middle-aged woman with her back turned to the counter was putting paper bands around stacks of money. She turned to face Melvin. With a look as if she smelled something bad, she asked, "How may I help you this morning?"

As Melvin walked up to the counter, the blond woman stepped back like she might catch something. Melvin replied, "Sorry. Do you handle Western Union?"

"No, we don't, but customer service is right next door. They can send a telegram for you.

There were quite a few people in line at customer service. When Melvin finally got up to the counter, he asked, "Ma'am, do you handle Western Union?"

With a sigh and moving little closer to the counter, the lady said, "Yes. Do you need to send a telegram?"

"No. My boss is supposed to wire me some money."

"Western Union is not really open yet, but I can check and see if there is a wire for you. Do you have a picture I.D.?"

"Yeah, the license is from Montana, but I have my Social Security card also."

"I'm not sure if I can accept that. I'll need to talk to the manager."

Melvin could feel his face getting hot and the collar of his shirt starting to feel tight around his neck. Starting to hyperventilate, he deliberately forced himself to slow his breathing. "That's fine. I can wait. Where is your manager?"

"He should be coming through those doors any minute. Actually I thought he would already be here."

In the meantime Darlene was browsing around the pharmacy area, and she was surprised to see Guaifenesin DM and Mucinex DM on the shelves. The last time she looked in other pharmacies, they were keeping them behind the counter.

It was early and there were no pharmacists or anybody else working in that area. It was almost too easy. She had her large handbag hanging off her shoulder. Looking right and left once more, she approached the shelves with the Mucinex and Guaifenesin. While sliding the bottles of pills in her handbag, she noticed Robitussin at the other end of the shelf. She threw several bottles into her bag.

A short fat balding man walked into the banking area and went behind the counter. The blond woman casually walked over to him, periodically looking up at Melvin then back at the bald man.

Walking slowly back to the counter, she motioned for Melvin to come to the counter. "My manager says that your license and Social Security card should be fine."

Darlene bent over the shelf with the Robitussin and scooped the entire shelf into her large handbag. She then saw and scooted to the shelf full of Vicks Nyquil and put them into her handbag. She casually looked up and saw no one.

Glancing over at Melvin as he counted money, she casually walked out of the store. She sensed more than saw someone behind her. Instinctively she headed away from the van.

Walking out of Walmart, Melvin noticed an Asian man, built short and wide, reminding him of a Samoan. The Samoan came up on Darlene. He grabbed her with thick stubby-fingered hands by the shoulder. Melvin didn't hear what he was saying, but he saw him reaching for handcuffs. Melvin moved quickly and silently. Pulling the Swiss Army knife out of his pocket, he moved directly behind the Samoan and with a thrust, drew the knife across his neck. The knife barely penetrated the Samoan's thick neck. As the short thick man turned, Melvin plunged the knife forward and forced the knife between his neck and his upper chest. Dark red, almost-black blood gurgled from his lips as the Samoan fell to the ground, but for an instant he managed to rise and grab for the knife. Melvin brought his right hand up and knocked the Samoan's hand away from his knife and pulled the knife out of the man's chest. As the Samoan started to get up again, Melvin moved quickly and jabbed the knife once again into the Samoan's torn bloody throat. The Samoan's hands came up to his throat. He covered his throat. Melvin could see coming out of his lips the blood trickling between his fingers. With a gurgle and blood, the Samoan fell to the asphalt parking lot. He put his hands up to his throat as the blood seeped through his thick fingers.

Looking carefully right then left and not seeing anyone in the parking lot, Melvin tried to drag the man to the edge of the parking lot near some low bushes. Two tries at dragging the Asian and barely being able to move the body. Darlene turned and tried to help. They gave up and left him lying in the deserted part of the parking lot.

"Okay, Darlene. What was that all about?"

Breathing heavily in between breaths, she said, "I think he may have been upset with me for taking the cough medicine."

"Okay, baby girl, we need to get, and fast. You don't think they knew we were together?"

"That's why I walked right past you. So they wouldn't know we was together."

As they headed north on Route 11, Darlene spoke up. "Melvin, do you know where we're goin? I think you're speeding."

"No, Darlene, I ain't speeding. But we do need to head north, and I do believe we are heading north."

"Ya think we could stop so I could get my Scat?"

"Let us get away from Slidell. There should be camp ground not far."

"Melvin, we still got that camping stove?"

The sun was getting brighter. Melvin could see steam coming off the road. "Yeah, the stove is back there with our sleeping bags."

Traffic appeared to be light as they drove. It was a relief for Melvin to have quiet. Darlene reached over to turn on the radio. There wasn't much of a selection on the FM stations. There was nothing but static on the stations. Back on the AM dial, she heard the sounds of an accordion and a fiddle, the announcer saying something about the best Cajun and Zydeco music in Southwestern Louisiana. Melvin just looked at her and then at the radio.

"Melvin, I still don't feel real good. I just needed somthen to distract me."

Looking back down at the radio and then at Darlene, he said, "That's all right. What did you get at the Walmart?"

"Got me some pills. Would you believe that they had these pills on the shelves?"

Letting out a long sigh, he asked, "What's so different about these pills?"

"They stopped putting these pills on the shelves a while ago. Now they have to keep them back in the pharmacy. As soon as you can find a place off the highway, I'll fix me some medicine."

"You can do that with those pills?"

"Yeah, but I need you to stop for a while so I can smash these pills. Then get some water and mix them real good."

Evening rush was just starting. The roads were not as crowded as expected. Leaning forward and squinting through the windscreen, he could see that it was getting dark and there were big black thunder clouds. Darlene had had her head back against the seat. Her mouth was open and there was drool running down her chin when she woke with a start. Wiping her chin with the back of her hand, she said, "Melvin, you're driving all over the road."

"I know the winds are picking up. You know this is what they call a high-profile vehicle. We need to get off the road."

As he turned the radio back on, he heard the announcer saying how they were to expect a storm, and tornados had been spotted in the area of Pearl River. "You know, Melvin, that's probably why there isn't that many people on the road. Seems like a weather warning has been put out."

Creeping over to the right side of the road, he said, "Darlene, there was a sign back there that said there is a rest area not far up the road." Just then Melvin pulled over on the shoulder of the road and made an abrupt stop. Sticking his head out of the window and looking back down the road, he put the van in reverse and drove about a half mile to the exit, stating that the next rest stop is twenty miles.

He backed down the shoulder of the highway. It started to sprinkle. Within seconds the sprinkle turned to large raindrops. The wind was gusting forcefully. It felt like they were at sea, as Melvin was trying in vain to keep the van on the shoulder of the road. The rains were now coming down with force. Melvin could barely see the entrance to the rest area. As he was pulling close to the public restrooms, he looked over toward Darlene, who hadn't uttered a word since he started backing down the highway. Her eyes were closed tight. Her lips were pressed together and rolled in so tightly that he barely saw them. Her cheeks were sucked in as if she were biting the inside. She was holding onto the handhold above the door so tightly that her knuckles were beyond white, almost purple. "Darlene! It's all right. Relax, I'm going to stop here until the storm stops."

He backed into a parking spot in front of a low rock wall in front of the public restrooms. Darlene turned quickly to see red and blue lights flashing. "Melvin, I think there's a cop coming right behind us."

Melvin pointed to the rear of the van. "Darlene, get in the back and stay quiet."

Just as Darlene was pulling a blanket up around her shoulders and lying down near the rear cargo doors, there was a knock from the back of a large flashlight on the driver's side window. Melvin cracked the window to see a man the size of a bear, a very large bear, with a wide brim, Smokey Bear-type hat with rainwater pouring off the brim, and wearing a bright yellow raincoat. "Yes, sir. What can I do for you?"

The trooper spoke with a deep thunderous voice, "Sir, could I see your license and registration?"

"Is there a problem, Trooper?"

"I don't think so. I just happen to see you backing up on the interstate." Squinting through the rain into the partially opened window, he asked, "Just what are you, boy?"

"What do you mean?"

"Are you Mexican? Maybe Puerto Rican?"

"No, sir. I'm Crow."

Scooting up on the seat and reaching into his back pocket for his wallet, he attempted to pull his license out. The trooper held up his hand. "You don't have to pull it out. Just let me look at it."

After seeing the ID that Melvin presented, the trooper said, "Wright don't sound like a Latino name."

"No, sir, I'm Crow."

"Oh, you mean you're some kind of Injun."

Taking a deep breath and looking up at the trooper, he said, "Sir, my registration is in the glove box."

"Is your proof of insurance in there too?"

"Yes, sir."

Shining his flashlight through the window toward the back of the van, he looked down at the license. "Mr. Wright, is someone in the back of the van?"

"Yes, sir. That's Darlene. She isn't feeling well. She's back there taking a nap."

"Can you call her up here?"

"Like I said, she is not feeling well. I think it's some kinda woman problem. She might have trouble climbing over the seat."

"You want to walk back with me and open those doors?"

"Yes, sir, but I'll need to pull up a little ways from that rock wall."

"Okay, Mr. Wright. Just keep your hands on the wheel until you move up a little."

Backing away from the van, the trooper started to walk to the back of the van.

With the rain dripping down from his Smokey Bear hat and face, he said, "Mr. Wright, stick your right hand out your window and slowly open your door."

Rolling his window down and leaning over to grab his keys, Melvin opened the door and eased himself out of the van. With the rain pounding on his face, Melvin attempted to look at the trooper. "I can't see anything. I'm coming around the left side of the van. I've got the keys to the van in my hand to unlock the cargo doors."

"It's all right, Mr. Wright. Sorry for any problems. We had a few complaints on this road. Take care of your wife. Be careful pulling out of here. You might want to stay here until the storm passes."

CHAPTER 5

It was a chilly morning, although the sun peeked through the cottonwood trees at the eastern edge of the property near the chain-link fence. Russell, with sweat running down his forehead and dripping off the end of his nose, diligently packed the trunk of the Caprice.

Naomi looked around the nearly empty street, noticing the boys running back and forth and around the house, apparently playing some kind of elusive game. She yelled, "Denny, Anthony, calm down now. See if you can help your dad." She looked around and saw Jacqueline standing in the middle of the empty asphalt street in front of their house with a thumb in her mouth, two fingers up her nose, just watching the boys.

With hands on her hips, Naomi yelled, "Jacquelyn, get out of the street."

Taking her thumb out of her mouth and her fingers out of her nose, Jackie said, "Mommy, me no in street."

"Okay, little miss, stay up here near me."

Shutting the trunk and looking up, Russell said, "All right. Everybody use the restroom. We won't be stopping for a while. I'd like to get as far as Biloxi by tonight."

"Jackie, Jackie, where are you?" called Naomi. She teetered up to the edge of the lawn and looked at her mother. "Let's put you into those diapers I bought for you. Just for the trip. You can have your pretty panties as soon as we get to Houston," Naomi remarked.

Pulling her thumb out of her mouth and removing her fingers from her nose, Jackie said, "No, Mommy. Me wear pretty panties."

"Okay, Jackie, but that means you have to act like a big girl."

As the car headed toward Highway 19, Naomi turned to Russell, "You know most people don't use 19 anymore."

"After all these years, you must know my sense of direction. If I know how to get someplace, I have to go that way every time. Maybe on the way back you can show me the new route. As of right now, you are my official navigator. Just let me get out of Florida the way I know."

* * *

Looking at the dashboard clock, Naomi tapped Russ on the shoulder. "It's getting close to noon. I've packed lunchmeat and bread in the cooler. Whenever you find a rest area, we can stop for lunch."

"I'd like to get as far as Pensacola," Russ said, opening and closing his hands. Holding the steering wheel with his left hand and then his right, then shaking his hands, he glanced over to Naomi. "Think you could massage my right hand? Feels like writer's cramp."

"You want me to take over for a while? Maybe after lunch I could do a little driving."

Breathing deeply, Russ said, "I'm all right. Just need to get a little circulation in my hands. We'll see after lunch."

They found a picnic table among the sea oats and snow white sands of Fort Walton beach. "You know, Russ, I'll never get tired of the mounds of snow white sand and the sea oats."

"Okay, kids, there are public restrooms"—Russ said, pointing back toward the road—"over there. You better go now. I don't really want to stop until we get past Biloxi."

* * *

From the backseat, Denny was whining. "When we gonna stop?"

Naomi turned her head to the backseat. "Denny? We just stopped for lunch less than"—looking at her wristwatch—"than an hour ago. Russ, are we going to stop for the night?"

Russ was having a little problem as the sun was setting directly in front of him. He glanced over at Naomi, whose head was down on her chest and who had just a little drool on her chin. "Naomi, Naomi, I need my navigator."

Shaking her head, wiping her mouth, and rubbing her eyes, Naomi asked, "What's the problem?"

"What else? I'm lost."

"Where are we?"

"Well, if I knew that, I would have let you sleep. We just crossed the Alabama state line. Do you think you could find the air base? We really don't have to go on base. I just thought I'd take a look-see."

"I can't say I can do much better, but this place does not look like the Biloxi we left. The only way I can find the base is by getting over on Highway 90, and then looking for White Avenue. I think I can find the main gate off U.S. 90. See, you're really not much different than me. I also have to find something I'm familiar with. When did they put the casinos on the beach? I remember that little Mexican pizza place. Guess it's gone."

"I tried to get us as close to the air force base as possible. I can't believe how much the air force has changed since I enlisted. I guess everybody is trying to be politically correct. I'm not sure I like the new air force," Russ remarked.

* * *

With the trunk open, Russ was putting their bags in the back. Looking over at Naomi, who was sitting on a chair in front of the Motel 6 and skimming through the pages of a magazine, Russ asked, "Naomi, have I got all our bags?"

"I just put our clothes in the dryer."

"We haven't been on the road a full day. We already need to wash clothes?"

"I've already washed the clothes. They're in the dryer. And yes, I needed to wash clothes. I'm not letting the grandparents see Jackie in a spaghetti-stained outfit. It's her favorite outfit."

"Okay, that should be it? It is, isn't it? Denny, go check the room make sure we haven't left anything behind?" inquired Russ.

Coming out of the room with Jackie in her arms, Naomi said, "I think that should do it. By the way, Russ, I know how you are with your coffee. I think I saw a donut shop as we turned off the interstate."

With Naomi behind the wheel, within a few minutes they had stopped at a donut shop. The Gallaghers were once again on the road. The kids were already coming down off a sugar high.

Tapping Naomi on the shoulder, he said, "Giving the kids donuts for breakfast may not have been one of our better ideas."

"Don't blame me for that."

"Well, I didn't hear any objections from you," Naomi replied.

The closer they got to the state line, the darker the skies got. As they came upon a bridge, Denny asked, "Daddy, is that the Mississippi River?"

"No, Denny. I'm not sure, but once we cross the Mississippi we should be in Texas. We're crossing into Louisiana right now. That could be the Pearl River. No, it's not. See that double span bridge. That's supposed to be the world's longest bridge. That's Lake Pontchartrain."

"Is that bridge longer than the Skyway?"

"Yes, Denny. Most of the Skyway Bridge is causeway."

Tapping Russ on the shoulder, Denny asked, "Are we gonna stop for lunch?"

"Yeah. I saw a sign that claims that the best food in the South is at the next exit. Which is five miles from here."

The sky was getting darker by the minute. It started with a light sprinkle, then a drizzle. As the raindrops got bigger, Anthony leaned over the seat and tapping his father on the shoulder, he said, "I really have to pee."

The rain was coming down in sheets, almost vertically. Leaning forward and squinting, Russ could barely see the exit sign. Less than a quarter mile off the highway, Naomi spotted what appeared to be the restaurant. Pointing to the right, she saw tractor trailers and at least a dozen cars.

Practically climbing over the seat, Anthony first grabbed his mom then his dad, whining, "No. Not there. I promise I can hold it. Please, we can't stop here."

Russ pulled the car off the road onto the shoulder just a few feet from the entrance to the restaurant. Everyone but Russ was staring at Anthony. "Why not, Anthony? Why can't we stop here?"

"Because this is a bad place."

"Why is this a bad place, Anthony?" asked Russ.

Crying now, Anthony whined. "Something real bad is going to happen here."

"Well, Anthony, we can stay in the car, but I have to stop. The rain is coming down so hard, I can't see the road. I think maybe you just scared yourself."

Looking back at Anthony, Naomi noticed, "Anthony, did you just pee your pants?"

"I'm sorry, Momma."

"Well," she said, once again looking down at Anthony's trousers, "we at least have to get you some dry pants and underpants."

Finding an open spot in front of the restaurant, Russell pulled in. Unbuckling his seat belt and turning and looking at his son, he said, "I guess I've been delegated to taking Anthony in and getting him changed." Everyone including Jackie just stared at Anthony.

"You take Anthony into the restroom and we'll find us a table. You want me to order you coffee?"

Anthony looked over at his mother. "That would be great."

"Not you, Anthony. I was talking to your father. By the way, are you still feeling bad about this place?"

"Yeah, I mean, yes, ma'am. But I guess we or I got us stuck here?"

"Okay. I'll see you guys inside."

Walking into the restroom area, Russ was assaulted by the odor of urine, reminding him of a garbage-strewn alleyway. Bending down and stiffing at Anthony's clothes, Russ concluded that the smell was not all his son's. Walking into the restroom, Russ saw four toilet stalls, six urinals, and four rust-stained sinks. Looking back at the door to make sure no one else was coming, Russ opened the bag that Naomi had given him with the change of clothes for Anthony.

There was no paper towels in the dispenser, but Anthony pointed to a trash can with a stack of paper towels sitting on top. Russ had Anthony take off his pants and underpants. Wetting several paper towels, he helped Anthony wipe himself down. The door to the restroom squeaked. Russ looked up to see a large heavyset man start to enter. When the man saw Russ and Anthony, the surprised man commented, "Sorry," and turned and left.

Russ called after him. "We'll be right out."

In contrast the dining area looked clean and neat. Naomi, Dennis, and Jackie, who was already in a high chair, were sitting at the far side of the dining room. Naomi spotted Russ and Anthony and waved them over to the table.

Anthony sat down next to his brother. Russ looked over at Naomi, holding the bag with Anthony's soiled clothes. "What do you think, Anthony? You want to get something to eat here?"

Reluctantly Anthony replied. "Yeah, yes, sir. I guess."

Holding the bag up, Russ said, "I'll take these out to the car."

Russ had carried something with him into the dining room. It was a large pink diaper bag hanging over his shoulder. Handing the bag to Naomi, he said, "I wasn't sure but I thought you might need this?"

Taking her thumb out of her mouth and her fingers out of her nose, Jackie said, "Jackie no want diaper."

"Do you want your sippy cup?"

With her thumb back in her mouth and shaking her head, Jackie replied, "Yeth."

"I would have completely forgotten about her sippy cup," Naomi replied, reaching for the bag.

"Well, did you guys order?"

"Daddy, I want chicken tenders. I guess that answers my question. What about you, Anthony. You want chicken tenders too?"

Looking up and taking a deep breath, Anthony said, "Can I get a chocolate milkshake?"

Looking over at Jackie, Naomi asked, "What about you, young lady. Do you want chicken tenders too?"

Shaking her head no and pulling her thumb out of her mouth, Jackie said, "Jackie want fried cheese. Where my bunny?"

Naomi wiped Jackie's hands. "You mean a grilled cheese sandwich? And I think I see your bunny sticking his head out of the bag. It **is** close enough to lunchtime."

"Well, my dear, I've heard you can eat breakfast any time. Working shift work for most my working life, I've been known to eat supper at six in the morning!"

Denny decided he would rather have sausage. Jackie had her pink bunny in one hand and her brother Anthony's chicken strips in the other.

After her second cup of coffee, Naomi looked at her daughter's with her sippy cup upside down. "Let me take Jackie to the restroom where I can wipe her hands and let her go potty." Turning and looking toward the big picture window next to the register, she said, "I think I actually see sunlight out there. It looks like the rain has stopped, at least for now."

Russ drained the last of his coffee. The boys were already standing, looking after their mother as she headed for the ladies room, "We'll meet you in the car. By the way, the men's was not that clean"

Standing next to the car, Russ announced, "Last chance to use the bathroom."

Denny looked over at Anthony. "We're all right. How much longer to Houston?"

"No more storms, and no traffic problems. We should be pulling onto Grandpa and Grandma's house in about four hours."

"Nooo!" That went right up Russell's spine. Then he heard the sound of a scream, "MOMMY... MOMMY!" Then silence.

The boys were looking at one another then their father. Denny spoke first, "Daddy. That was Jackie."

"Boys. Stay right here. Get in the car and lock the doors. Don't open the door until I get back."

Running and pushing open the door to the ladies room, Russ looked down to see his wife on the floor bleeding from her mouth, her hair matted with blood, and unconscious. As he knelt down beside her, the door to the ladies room opened and the waitress who served them was standing above him. With her hands on her hips, the waitress looked down at Russ. "What is going on here?"

"I heard a scream and found my wife laying here in a pool of her own blood. She was with my daughter."

Just then Naomi opened her eyes and started to yell. "Where is my baby?"

Looking at the waitress, Russ said, "Please stay with her." He ran to the door and looked out just in time to see a dark blue cargo van spitting up mud and gravel, sliding on the loose gravel, the wheels spitting more dirt, mud, and gravel as it fishtailed onto the highway.

Naomi was sitting up when Russ returned to the restroom. The waitress was just standing there staring at Naomi. Russ turned to the waitress. In an authoritative voice, he said, "Call the police and tell them this is an emergency."

A trooper was sitting across from Russ and the boys in a corner booth. Naomi was sitting at a chair across from the booth with an ice pack on her head. Looking up at Naomi, the state trooper asked, "Ma'am, let me call the ambulance for you?"

Naomi started to shake her head then moaned, "**Aweee!** No, I can't go to the hospital. I need my baby."

The trooper sitting in the booth with Russ and the boys looked at Russ and then at Naomi. "I'm Senior Trooper Thibodeaux. Trooper Jackson is looking around the ladies room. Mrs. Gallagher, you really should have someone look at that."

Russell's head was in his hands, his eyes red and swollen. Anthony was crying. Denny was doing all he could do to keep from crying.

With effort Russell lifted his head and looked directly at the senior trooper. "I need to know what you are doing about getting our child back."

Thibodeaux looked over at Russell, "Sir, I've radioed it in and there are people looking right now. Did you happen to notice a license plate?"

"Sorry. I know it was not a Louisiana tag."

Anthony looked up to see a state trooper with Jackie's pink bunny in his hand. "Daddy, that's Jackie's bunny."

A tall thin black trooper walked up to Russ. Putting the hand with the stuffed rabbit out and handing it to Russ, he said, "I'm Trooper Jackson— Greg Jackson. I found this on the floor." Looking over at Senior Trooper Thibodeaux, he said, "I checked every stall, took pictures of the crime scene. I dusted what I could for prints, at least the flat surfaces. We're not going to get prints off the stuffed rabbit."

"Thank you, Jackson. Did you radio the barracks?"

"Yes, sir. They are calling headquarters and there will be a team sent out, including the forensic guys."

The senior trooper stood up and looked down at Russ. "Are you staying close by?"

Looking up and directly into the senior trooper's cat's eyes, "No, sir. We were on our way to Houston to visit with my folks."

Thibodeaux looked over at the boys and then at Russ. "We'll take it from here. We need you guys to stay close. Do you have a cell phone?" Russell shook his head no.

Naomi replied, "I have a cell phone."

Thibodeaux continued, "Let me know where you will be staying. We'll call you as soon as we set up. We will set up near you and will be monitoring your phone. We will keep you informed of our progress, and as soon as we find something out we will tell you."

Naomi looked up at the senior trooper and with red swollen eyes and a voice that sounded as if her sinuses where totally congested, she said, "I am not leaving until you find my baby. I want my baby back right now." Her head was down, both her hands at her temples. It started with a mumble hardly heard by anyone, then there was a sound that seemed to come from deep within her. She stood up and reaching for the senior trooper, she grabbed his collar and started pounding on his chest while yelling, "**NO, NO!** My baby is gone! I need you to do your job and bring my baby home."

She continued pounding on the trooper's chest. Russ went to her and grabbed her shoulders. He then put his arms around her waist, and using all his strength, he was finally able to pull her away from the senior trooper and through sheer force of will had her sit next to him.

Motioning to the waitress, Russ indicated that he wanted her to bring a glass of water.

Jackson turned to face Naomi. "We are doing everything we can. You can't stay here in this restaurant. There is a motel not far from here. It's very reasonable. Our detectives are on their way. They're coming up from Baton Rouge. That's not that far away." Turning to the senior trooper and then at the Gallaghers, Jackson in a low calm voice stated, "The FBI has been notified and they will also be here."

A tall man with a three-day-old gray growth of whiskers, wearing a stained apron, walked over to Naomi, "Ma'am, I am so very sorry. There is really nothing I can say. I've owned this place for over twenty years. We've had our share of rowdy customers. Been robbed couple times, but this has never happened before." At the same time Cheryl was motioning to Thibodaux. "I've locked the doors and put the close sign up.

"So ifen you need to stay a while it be all right with us. By the way, I'm Karl," the man with the stained apron added.

With red swollen eyes, Russell looked up at Karl. "I do appreciate all your kindness. Ya know, I was eaten' sand and dodgen' bullets for the last eighteen months. I really thought the worse was over. Karl, thank you and Cheryl for all your help."

Russell looked over at his wife. She was sitting at the edge of a cushioned seat at the corner the booth. He noticed she had a weird look about her. She was just staring into space. Karl reached out a hand to Russell. At that moment Naomi stood. As she was getting up, her hands came up to her temples and she fell flat on her face. Not even trying to protect her face, she landed directly on her nose, which was now bleeding profusely.

Trooper Jackson's eyes became round orbs as he reached for his radio. Looking over at the senior trooper, he said, "I think we really need to get an ambulance here.

Two men banged on the door. Karl went to the door and examined their badges. Russell noticed it wasn't at all like the movies. They were both wearing jeans. The taller one had a sweatshirt on, and the short blond-haired man was wearing a western shirt with a bow tie and a turquoise and silver tie clip up near his throat.

Denny was the first to notice the reddish-brown cowboy boots on the shorter detective. Looking down at the boots and then up at his father, he said, "Daddy, I ain't never seen boots like that."

The short blond one with the cowboy boots just grinned at Denny then looked down on the floor at Naomi. Squatting down next to her, he reached down and helped her sit up. "Can you sit up? I mean do you feel like you are going to pass out again?"

Putting her hands back up at her temples, she said, "I just have the mother of all headaches." She felt the blood from her nose going down her throat and she started coughing. Grabbing a handful of napkins, the detective with the shiny boots handed them to Naomi. "Gently, very gently, blow your nose. Not too hard. You don't want to get the bleeding started again.

"Just lean back against the booth. We got a limousine coming for you."

* * *

Just as the detective said that, two men with a stretcher entered the door. Two more men entered. The shorter white-haired man was wearing a brown suit with a subdued tie. The other man was tall, very tall, and was in a charcoal suit with a red tie. Both had military-style haircuts. Russell thought the shorter man's hair was almost as white as snow. The taller man's hair color was nondescript, maybe a mousy brown or sandy. *What in the world am I thinking? My wife is laying on the floor with a bloody nose, my two boys look like zombies, and my daughter has been stolen, and I am trying to describe FBI agents?*

Trooper Jackson walked over to Russell. "If you'd like, you can follow the ambulance to the hospital. The senior trooper and I will brief the detective and the agents. We all know where to find you."

The trip to the hospital was uneventful, except that Russell had to find his way back to the restaurant. Russ could hear the muffled crying of his two boys. Anthony, still holding the pink bunny rabbit tightly in his hand, leaned up against the front seat. "Daddy, I am so sorry. We **will** get Jackie back."

Leaning his head back, Russ said, "I know, Anthony. We will. Now let's check on your mom."

Naomi was taken into the emergency room where there were several people standing over her. The last thing Russell saw as they were escorting him out of the little room in the ER was a lot of shiny instruments near Naomi's nose. As he was leaving the room, a woman in green scrubs entered with what looked like gauze and disinfectant. Sitting in a chair in the hallway not far from the room that Naomi was in, he saw a man with a gurney heading for Naomi's room. It just dawned on him that he didn't know where his boys where. Walking to the entrance to the ER and looking through the small glazed windows, he could make out his boys sitting on what looked like overstuffed couches watching TV.

He stood up as he saw the gurney with his wife on it pass him. Calling out to the two people in surgical gowns that were pushing the gurney, he said, "Where are you taking her?"

The two men in suits with the white-walled military-style haircuts came up to Russ. The shorter of the two handed Russ a card. "I'm Special Agent in charge Asa Williams." Pointing to the man in the charcoal suit, he said, "This is Special Agent Walton."

Two men in white lifted Naomi onto the gurney and put her in the back of an ambulance.

Looking over at Russell's red swollen eyes, Special Agent Williams motioned for Russell to follow the ambulance. "Mr. Gallagher, it is Gallagher? You can follow the ambulance. We'll be along shortly."

A woman wearing white slacks and a white blouse following the gurney turned to Russell and replied, "She should be fine. They want to get an MRI just to make sure there's no swelling on her brain and to check for any other damage."

"Can I go down there with you?"

The nurse lifted her head and turned to him. "Sure."

CHAPTER 6

Fishtailing out of the restaurant parking lot, Melvin looked over at Darlene. Her head was on her chest and she was drooling. He pulled the van off the road behind three Spanish moss-draped oaks. After pulling behind some of the higher scrub bushes, he walked around to the cargo doors and very slowly and quietly opened the cargo doors. He climbed up next to Jackie. He jerked her hair and, with his big hands, stroked her red locks. He seemed fascinated with her hair. She knew he was talking to her because she heard his voice, his words, but she couldn't distinguish anything coherent in them. She had stopped crying. She was now just whimpering. She could still hear him talking. She didn't want to listen to anything he had to say anyway. He was pulling at her panties. She was kicking and tried to scream. He put one hand over her mouth. She bit his little finger. He hit her with the back of his hand across her face. She was squirming. He was having trouble holding her hands still. He once again tried put his dirty hands over her mouth. This time she bit his thumb, drawing blood. He pulled his hands away and, with the back of his hand, he smacked her. For Jackie, everything went black.

Just then Darlene woke. Turning she yelled. "What's going on back there?"

Sliding out the cargo doors, Melvin answered, "Just trying to get this kid to shut up. I think she was about to go into convulsions. I tried to restrain her but she bit me."

* * *

Melvin was now once again behind the steering wheel. "Darlene, will you shut that kid up?"

Jackie was no longer crying or screaming. Every rugged breath just caused her to whimper. Looking down at her purple face, Darlene was sure the little girl was about to go into convulsions and die. "Melvin, what did you do to this baby?"

"I smacked her and not that hard."

"Yes, Melvin, she has a bruise on her face. We better not let anyone see her."

The rain had stopped, but the windshield was muddier than it was. While they used the windshield wipers, the mist spray just spread the mud over the windshield, making it even harder to see. Melvin reminded Darlene of a dog hanging his head out of the window. In a shaky voice, Darlene asked again, "Melvin, we have to wash the windshield."

"Can't stop until we cross the state line. Hey, that kid is awful quiet. What did you do?"

"I still had a little Nyquil. She liked it. Ya know it tastes like cherry syrup."

"**Damn!** Darlene, she's just a baby. That could kill her. This kid is worth a lot of money. She ain't worth nutten' if she's dead."

"I'm sorry, Melvin, but she **is** sleepen'."

"You just better hope that she wakes up."

Squatting in the cargo area of the van, Darlene tapped Jackie on the shoulder. Getting frustrated, she shook her. Jackie did not appear to be waking up. "Wake up. Wake up, little one." Taking a deep breath, she shouted, "**Melvin!** I can't get her to wake up. I think I killed her."

Still trying to see through the muddy windshield, Melvin yelled back. "Darlene! Is she breathing?"

"Yeah."

"Is her breathing deep and steady or very light?"

"She's breathing deep and steady, but I can hear a rattle when she breathes."

"Well, just let her sleep. At least she has finally stopped her crying."

Climbing over the seat next to Melvin, with a grunt and groan, Darlene sat down. Turning to Melvin and pointing to a road sign, Darlene said, "Melvin, that sign says we're heading toward Jackson. Isn't Jackson in Mississippi?"

"Yeah, it is. We got to go this way to get home."

"Yeaa… But don't I… don't we have to go west. Last I checked Mississippi was east."

"I know, Darlene, but we got to go this way to get that way."

"Well, we got to stop soon."

"Why? The gas gauge tells me we got more than half a tank. You got your medicine earlier."

"It's the kid. She stinks. I found a change of clothes in the diaper bag. We got to get someplace where I can clean her up."

He stared at Darlene while roaming onto the shoulder of the road. The tires spat up gravel. Melvin turned abruptly, almost losing control as the van slid, kicking up gravel and dirt. "Okay, Darlene. I need to clean these windows… Aw, what is that smell?"

"I told you I need to clean the kid."

"Keep an eye open for Mile Marker 72. There should be restrooms there."

"I think she's waking up. Don't think she's going to be doing that much crying. Maybe a little whimpering. She just says she wants Mr. Bunny."

"What the hell does that mean?"

"She keeps opening and closing her hands. I think it's some kind of stuffed animal. **Over there**."

"Over there what?"

"The mile marker and it looks like they got toilets."

"You need to find out her name. I mean people are going to notice if we don't know what to call her."

Turning into the rest area, Melvin said, "Aw, shit!"

"What's the matter?"

"Unless it's Christmas, those blue and red blinking lights mean cops. Just get back there with the kid and keep her quiet." Melvin turned to his open window as the policeman walked up to his car, standing at least two feet back from the door.

With his large flashlight, the police officer banged on the side of the van. "Sir, would you please put your hands on the steering wheel?"

"Yes, sir. What seems to be the problem?"

"Is there anyone else in the van?"

"Yes, sir. My woman and kid are in the back. The kid has been complaining about a bellyache."

Walking up to the window, the police officer stepped away from the van and shone his light to the back of the van. "Ma'am, could you lift up your hands, open your hands, and turn your palms toward me?"

Darlene lifted up her hands and looked down at Jackie. "Honey, you just try and be quiet?"

"Thank you, ma'am. You can put your hands down. Sir, using your right hand, would you open the door and step out?"

"Yes, sir. Is there a problem?"

"Sir, you seemed to be having trouble keeping your van on the road. Would you come out here and take a little walk for me?"

"Yes, sir. I got a bum leg."

"Well, you can either walk the line for me or I can call the police van and have the paramedics take a little blood sample."

With a smile and squinting against the reflection of the sun in the police officer's mirrored sunglasses, he said, "Yes, sir. I'll try walking for you."

Dark clouds started to cover the sun. Melvin felt droplets of water on his face. The wind picked up and the rain was no longer just a few droplets. It had started to come down steadily. Opening the door slowly, Melvin slid out of the van. Melvin walked away from the policeman then toward the policeman. His tee shirt was drenched. Melvin started to shiver as the wind picked up from the north. "Anything else, officer?"

"One more thing. Lift up your right leg and put your finger on your nose."

Melvin stood there with water starting to drip off his nose for what seemed like five minutes with his right leg up and his index finger on his nose. He was sure he was going to fall flat on his face. The sound of a crying child got both their attentions. With water starting to cascade off his wide-brimmed hat, the police officer said, "I'm sorry, sir, but I followed you for about five miles and you seemed to be having trouble keeping your van on the road. I hear your child in there." Looking at the muddy windshield, he said, "While you're here, you need to wash that windshield. If you can see well enough to drive, there is a gas station a couple miles down on the right side. Take the next exit and the gas station is just off to your right. No wonder you were having a problem keeping the van on the road. I'm going to give you a warning. As long as you keep your van on the road and stay within the speed limit, you'll be okay. Now take care of that child. By the way, is that a little boy or a little girl? She sounds like she's got the croup or somthen'."

"Yeah, we need to get her home. Seems like she has a little congestion." The rain was now pouring off the brim of the officer's hat like a waterfall.

"You say you've got a little girl back there? What's her name?"

"Her name is a… Sara, but she probably wouldn't recognize it. We've been calling her Snookum since before she was born."

Pushing his hat back and scratching his head, he held his hat against the wind. With his head down against the wind, the police officer climbed into his cruiser. Melvin could see the trooper pick up the mike. He put the mike back on the radio. Leaning out the partially opened window, he waved with his thumb up at Melvin. Rolling the window back up, Melvin turned back to his steering wheel, turned off the lights, and pulled out onto the highway.

Opening the cargo doors, Darlene stepped out with Jackie. Melvin cupped his hands against the wind and rain and lit up a cigarette. He inhaled deeply and let the smoke out slowly.

Halfway to the restrooms, Darlene turned toward Melvin. "Are we gonna be all right?"

"Yeah. I watched him on the radio. If he had a problem, he wouldn't have pulled away and we would be seeing a lot more cops."

With the van's cargo doors open and holding Jackie in her arms, Darlene was moving their camping gear, lifting up the sleeping bags with the hand not holding the little girl, and ripping through her large handbag. "Melvin, get over here and hold this kid!"

She dumped the bag's contents on the floor of the van. "I can't find it!"

"You can't find what?"

"None of it."

"Darlene, what are you talking about?"

"The Scat."

"You mean what we just scored?"

"Yeah, the Scat and the syringes. I talked to those people outside the meth clinic. Somebody gave me a few syringes. Now they're gone."

"Darlene, did you just throw it out the door?"

"No, Melvin. It has to be that kid. Leave her here. We definitely do not need her getten' in my shit."

"Darlene, you're wrong. Larry has already advanced us several thousand dollars. We got to get the kid up to the house. You and I have a little work to do. We need to train her."

"Train her? What do you mean train her?"

"We got to get her to stop crying. Tell her that her mother is dead or somum."

"We can't do that. She's a little girl, and I don't know how much she knows."

"Well, if I can train a puppy, I think the two of us can train one little girl."

"Melvin, when I train a dog, I use a newspaper."

"Well, we do the same thing with the kid. When she doesn't do what we want, just smack her with a rolled-up newspaper. Let's try that and see if we can get her name.

"Okay, Darlene. We'll be coming up on a pretty good-sized city. I'm pretty sure we've got enough money to get your Scat there. I been here before. There's a sports bar not far from the exit. There used to be a dealer that would hang out there. I can't think of his name."

"When we stop for you to wash the windshield, remind me to pick up a nice thick newspaper."

"Hey, Darlene, what do you feed a kid?"

"Imagine she eats like any human being."

* * *

Looking into the setting sun and coming around the loop surrounding the city for the third time, Melvin was irritated and frustrated and glanced over at Darlene. "I know where we need to go. I can see the neighborhood from here. What I don't know is how to get off this damn loop circling the city. I told you I'd take you to visit Elvis."

"Just take the first exit close to where you think we need to be."

"I see an exit. Who puts an exit on the left side of the road?"

At the next exit, Melvin pulled the van off the road. Driving into an area of boarded-up stores and run-down empty tenements, he saw black teenagers standing on a corner next to a store with windows so dirty that he couldn't tell if it was a store and if it was open. Might be just an old abandoned building.

As he pulled over to the curb next to the building with the darkened dirty picture window, a very large muscular black teenager wearing a long black trench coat walked up to the to the side of the van. "What you doen' here?"

Melvin turned thinking, *It is hot out here and this kid is wearing a trench coat.* He turned toward the teenager. "Last time I was here there was a sports bar down here someplace."

The teenager reached into one of the pockets of the trench coat. Melvin felt that familiar feeling in the pit of his stomach. The same feeling that kept him alive and making sure he was no one's bitch while in prison. The teenager brought his hand out of his pocket with a pack of cigarettes and held the pack out to Melvin. Melvin grabbed one and while he was lighting the cigarette, the teenager came up with a knife in his hand. As the kid brought up the hand with the knife and struck at the open window, Melvin brought his hand down hard on the kid's wrist and in one motion brought his knife up and put it through the kid's right hand, casually pushing the knife midway in the kid's hand. The kid screamed but muffled the scream in a matter of seconds. The knife dropped to the inside of the open window. "Now, as I was saying, is that sports bar anywhere near here?"

With a very high-pitched voice for a very large boy, the kid replied, "No, sir." The kid looked down at his hand. "Please, please, pull your knife out of my hand." The kid tried to pull his hand but managed to let out another yelp. "There was a bar like that, but like everything else around here, it be boarded up. Iffen you need weed or blow I can help."

"I want Scat. I've been chasing the dragon for the last day. The word is I can get what I need here."

Melvin pulled the knife out of the kid's hand then grabbed his hand. With pressure, he held it tight, looking directly in the kid's dark brown bloodshot eyes, then looking down to see blood dripping from the kid's hand onto his pants. Pushing the kid's hand back, he said, "I don't know, kid. Is there anyone around here that can help me score Smack?"

"All I got is blow and weed."

"If you haven't noticed, I'm not all that pleased with you."

"Ya, yes, sir, I noticed. I'm going to reach in my pocket." Melvin gave him a stare and let go of his hand. "I'm just pullen' out my phone. I know someone who can get you what you want. You got the green?"

The kid started to turn. Melvin popped the door of the van open and grabbed the kid's wrist. "You callen' your supplier?"

"Yes, sir."

"You can stay right here while you call."

"The man don't like meeten' new people."

"Well, you just tell him if he wants the sale, he'll meet me here."

"How do I know you ain't the man?"

"Well, you don't. But if you don't get me what I want, your momma ain't even goin' a recognize you."

The kid rubbed his hand and looked to his right and his left. Looking for his bros and seeing the street empty, he said, "Okay."

Melvin looked back down the deserted street to see a short skinny old black man with short cropped gray hair, wearing clean pressed khakis and a blue striped tee shirt walking toward him. As the man approached and looked directly at him, Melvin looked down to see that the man was wearing sandals. "You the one that took me away from the ball game? Open your shirt. Now come closer. Drop your pants."

Melvin reached for his belt. Then, looking over at the old black man, he said, "I bet you're not even going to take me out to dinner?"

"Pull you pants up. I don't need to see your junk. Now what do you want?"

"I need brown, snow or whatever in other words like I told your boy here, I need to make a buy."

"Not much tonight. Maybe just little more than a taste, but I'll have more tomorrow. Now let me see the green."

Melvin opened his hands and said, "I'm goen' a reach in my pocket." He pulled out a roll of bills. "Ya know, I been thinken'. Maybe I need to go someplace else to get what I need?"

"If you got the green"—he said, looking at the wad in Melvin's hand— "I can maybe get you a tenth of a gram."

"Okay. Here's the deal. You sell me a gram, I'll give you a C note."

"You got it with you? You willin' to pay that much?" The black man shook his head. "Okay. You got a sale."

Digging in his pocket, the old man pulled out two square-shaped aluminum foil packets.

Melvin turned to his van, carefully opened the two packets, and put the powder on a wet index finger to taste it, after which he refolded the packets. "Thank you, sir, it has been a pleasure doing business with you."

Climbing back in the van, Melvin looked back into the cargo area. Seeing, more like hearing, Darlene and the kid taking turns snoring, he did notice a little whimper, almost like a puppy, out of the little girl. The heat was becoming oppressive.

Darlene was climbing over the seat as he made an exit onto the highway. Putting her face next to the air-conditioning vent, she let out a sigh and fanned herself with the rolled-up newspaper. "Where are we going now?"

Handing Darlene two square aluminum-wrapped packets, he said, "You got any syringes?" She shook her head. "Darlene, we are going home." Pointing to the packets in her hand, he said, "That had better last." The sky was getting darker. The drizzle had turned to rain. Thunder could be heard in the distance. The wind was now once more coming in from the north, becoming colder.

* * *

The sky was even darker as they crossed into the Dakotas. They had driven out of the heavy rain, but the light drizzle was freezing on the windshield. Melvin turned on the heat. He spotted the lights of a diner coming up on the left side of the single-lane blacktop. He yelled. "Darlene, wakey-wakey. Come on, Darlene, wake up. I gotta get some coffee, maybe even somthen' to eat."

Sitting in a booth at the far corner of the truck stop dining room, Darlene glanced over at Melvin. "Think I want a cheeseburger. Think the kid will eat a cheeseburger?"

"Don't know what little rugrats eat. Heard they've been known to eat crayons."

"No, Melvin. We are not feeding the kid crayons."

A sound—more like a mumble—came from the kid. Darlene looked over at Melvin. "Did you hear that?"

This time it was clear, "Jackie want hamburger."

"Okay. **Now** we know how to get the kid to behave," replied Melvin.

Melvin just shook his head as he stared at Jackie. Her mouth was already full and chomping steadily, as the hamburger bun lay in pieces on the high-chair tray.

* * *

Darlene knew the Black Hills were close, but they were hidden by dark clouds and rain. The windshield wipers were on the high setting. The rain was so thick at times that the van's headlights just reflected the light, making the road almost impossible to see.

They had been driving for a few hours and were getting close to home. The rain had all but stopped. Light snow flurries were now taking the place of rain. The sky lit up with a strike of lightning and a crash of thunder. The snow flurries were now large snowflakes. Melvin seemed to be hitting puddles and potholes on the narrow street. Passing boarded-up store fronts and finally turning onto an icy snow-covered road, Melvin could barely see his double-wide. The snow drift in front of the trailer was at least five feet deep. Melvin knew there was a driveway. There were also drainage ditches near the side of the road. The ditch and the driveway were covered in snow. Melvin got out of the van, worked his way to the back, and using the shovel they had found in Louisiana, wandered the front lawn like a blind man with a white cane. After finding the driveway, he cleared enough snow to see worn tracks off the driveway. After slipping and sliding, he finally managed to get onto the driveway and close to the trailer.

Darlene slid out of the back of the cargo van, reaching back to pick up her handbag and Jackie. Jackie's head flopped to the side as Darlene picked her up. "Melvin, this child is burning up." Jacquelyn made a little grunt as Darlene walked toward the double-wide. Turning back toward Melvin, she said, "Someone tacked an envelope to the door."

Yelling from the van, he asked, "What does it say?"

"It's too dark and way too cold. I can't even feel my fingers."

Trying to balance Jackie in one arm and inserting the key with the other hand, she stooped down and squinted, then put her frozen fingers on the lock. Trying again to insert the key, she said, "Melvin, I can't get the key in the lock. Would you shine your flashlight on the lock?"

Shining the flashlight on the door lock, he asked, "Does that help?"

"I think the lock is frozen."

"Okay. You and the kid get back in the van. I'll see if I can heat up the lock, which can actually sometimes make it worse."

Climbing in the back of the van, Jackie was sweating and shaking. Darlene wrapped her in one of the blankets in the back of the van and put her in a sleeping bag. Jackie looked up at Darlene and vomited. "Oh shit. How gross," was Darlene's response.

Trying to jiggle the key into the lock, Melvin was afraid to twist the key too hard. *All I need now is to break the key off in the lock.* "What's a matter, Darlene?"

"Oh, Melvin, the kid just puked all over me."

"Woo."

"Woo? I just said the kid puke all over me."

"I got the door open. The lights seem to be working. I'll turn the water heater up. You can clean up."

Putting Jackie on the couch, she looked over at the kitchen table and saw the envelope. "Well, Melvin, are you going to open the envelope?"

"Yeah. Let me get the circulation back in my hands."

"Here, give it here." As she tore the envelope open, several bills fell on the floor. "Somebody left us some money."

"Must be from Larry. He wasn't supposed to be here until tomorrow. Darlene, you read the note. The feeling is just coming back in my hands." He handed the note to Darlene.

"Says he was early and was hoping the package was ready for shipping. It's signed Labeeb. What's Labeeb?"

"That's Larry. I just feel funny calling him Labeeb."

Undressing Jackie, Darlene noticed that her skin was almost blue. There seemed to be a rash all over her body. When she breathed, Darlene could hear a gurgling and a squeaky, wheezing sound coming from Jackie. "Melvin, this child is so hot it feels as if she is going to burn my hands."

"Well, we don't have any aspirin. Get her in the shower and run the cold water."

"Then what?"

"While you're cleaning you and her up, I'll start the van. We're taking her to the hospital."

"The clinic's closed. The ambulance with the EMTs should be there, but she needs a doctor."

"I know that. I said we were taking her to the hospital. I don't think Larry can pay me enough for this."

CHAPTER 7

Naomi was being hustled, first to X-ray where she was put in a tunnel. More waiting. She was taken into a small examining room where a small section of her head was shaved and a nurse put sutures in that small shaved portion of her head. The wound was deep and it took three stitches. Russ and Naomi waited in another small room, leaving Naomi lying back on an examining table. Finally a man identifying himself as Dr. Abadi said, "I would like very much to"—looking down at Naomi—"have you stay here for the night."

Naomi, sitting up, just stared at the doctor.

"Very well. It looks as if you bruised your nose. The nose is not broken. However, you will probably wake up with two black eyes. From what I can see, there is no swelling, except for your nose. I have no doubt you have a mild concussion. When you get home, put a cold compress on you face. Just your eyes and nose. I'll prescribe a mild pain reliever. I think I will give you a mild sedative. You must wait until you get home to take the sedative. I would also like for you to stay awake for a while, so wait for at least an hour before you take the sedative. You are not driving, are you?"

Russell looked out into the waiting area to check on his boys. "Doctor, I am now confused. First, you tell me to give her a sedative when we get home. Now you say to wait an hour and keep her awake."

Rubbing his eyes, the doctor replied, "Yes, that is correct."

Shaking his head, he helped Naomi off the examining table and motioned to the boys to follow him. With a sigh, Russell gestured for the boys to come over and help him get their mother in the car. Helping Naomi bend her head down, he said, "Naomi, watch your head."

Just as Russell was about to climb into his car, his heart felt as if it would stop as he felt a tap on his shoulder. Turning abruptly, he saw the FBI agent with the snow white hair—a man who was actually slightly shorter than Russell, with white hair that reminded Russ that if it weren't for his ruddy complexion, he would look like his son Anthony. "You scared the shit out of me."

"Sorry." He handed his card to Russ. "We met at the restaurant. My partner, Special Agent Walton, and I walked in as your wife was being carried out on a stretcher."

"I really didn't notice much."

Rubbing his jaw, he said, "Well, I am Agent Asa Williams, and the agent in charge. We, Agent Walton and I, were just about to ask a few questions when they carried your wife to the hospital. First, let me tell you how sorry I am about what you have been through. The troopers gave us a very good report, so I won't ask you to go through it again, unless you can think of anything else. I would like to ask your wife a few more questions. It would be better if I could do it now, but I don't think she is in any shape right now. So I would like to come by in the morning."

"I don't even know where I'll be in the morning."

"We presumed to arrange two rooms for you in the motel across the street from the restaurant. Our friendly federal government will cover your expenses." Looking up at Russ, he said, "You do know I am being sarcastic? Anyway I'd appreciate you not tell my supervisors as they really lack a sense of humor. Anyway I'll give you a call in the morning."

Looking into the car and then at the agent, he started, "Agent…"

Looking up at Russ, the agent said, "I know you weren't expecting to be staying here. If there is anything else I can do for you, please let me know."

"I really have to get my wife and kids some place to rest."

"If you were wondering, we have a very good working relationship with the state and local authorities."

"Where is this motel?"

"Right across the street from the restaurant." He scratched his head. "Sorry. Just follow me."

"Detective, I don't know how much sleep any of us will get, but could you at least wait until the sun rises?"

"Yes, sir. Speaking of getting in touch, do you happen to have a cellular phone?"

"No, but my wife does."

The street lights were giving Russ a headache. The drive back to the highway didn't really take that long.

Watching the detective enter the office, Russ thought, *I wonder how tall he really is without the boots?*

Russell's head was back on the seat rest when Agent Asa Williams tapped on the window of the car. "Mr. Gallagher, could I borrow your wife's phone? It will only take a few minutes. Your rooms are on the second floor." Russ put his hand out to retrieve the keys to their rooms. Looking up he noticed a navy blue, full-sized van slow down and then park next to the office of the Sun Downer Motel in Slidell, Louisiana. Four men dressed in different navy blue polo shirts, tan tactical pants, and combat boots sat inside the van. With practiced expertise, the burly men with crew cuts set up a small dish antenna.

Asa looked over at his partner and with his hands motioned that he would be a few minutes longer. "Mr. Gallagher, that van has listening devices in it. We will be monitoring your cell phone. You may not believe this now but that van will become unobtrusive once they are completely set up."

"Yes, I do believe you. I've spent many hours in the Syrian Desert doing the very same thing."

"Well, that van belongs to the FBI. Those four burly men with crew cuts belong to the FBI. Give me a few minutes with your phone. I'll bring it back to you shortly."

While Agent Williams was going over the van, Russ was trying to help his wife up the stairs to their rooms. The first couple of steps went well, but

Naomi started to stagger. She almost fell when Agent Walton appeared to catch her.

* * *

"Hey, Dad, me and Anthony have our own room."

Helping Naomi to one of the two large queen-sized beds, Russ said, "Look again, boys. There's a door that opens right into my room. We will keep that door open."

Reaching into her purse, Naomi pulled out Jackie's pink bunny and placed it on the dresser. "Oh, Russ, what am I going to do? Strangers have got my baby."

"From the looks of things, they have all the law enforcement agencies here in the parking lot."

Just then Anthony came running into the room, "Daddy, I am sorry. We will get Jackie back, I promise."

Plopping down on the other bed and beckoning for Anthony, Russ said, "Anthony, it is not your fault, but you are right, we will get Jackie back."

It really wasn't that hot. As a matter of fact, it was getting cool, if not cold, outside. Russell heard the heat kick on. He was lying on the other queen-sized bed alone. He had the sheets pulled down, but he was in his underwear on top of the sheets with his arm across his eyes listening to his wife's moans and deep breathing in the other bed.

He may have dozed off for a few minutes. The sun was coming through the blinds. Naomi was standing by the window with what looked like a small glass of iced tea. He threw his legs on the floor before sitting up. Upon standing, he walked over to his wife. Putting a hand on her shoulder, he asked, "Where did you get the iced tea?" As he moved up closer, he realized it was not iced tea. He could smell the booze. "Where did you get the booze?"

"While you were asleep, I went down to the office and asked the night clerk where I could get a drink. He told me to wait." She took a large swallow of the amber beverage. "I don't know where he went, but he was gone for about five minutes and sold me this," she said, holding up a pint-sized bottle.

"Whiskey?"

Turning back to the window, she held one of the blinds up and peered outside at the parking lot. "No, Russ, it's actually bourbon. I was going to buy a Coke, but the machine is right outside our door. Thought it would make too much noise, and I didn't want to wake you. I started with a little ice and water. I still have ice and I don't need any more water."

Looking over at the dresser and seeing Jackie's pink bunny, Naomi walked over to the dresser and picked it up. Putting her face on the bunny and sniffing, she started to cry. Between sobs, she said, "You know, Russ, I thought the bourbon might numb me or at least let me sleep. No such luck."

Putting his arms around her, he said, "Naomi, is that going to help your headache?"

Walking back to the window, she replied, "Russell, I don't know, but I thought the numbness might help."

Pulling one of the blinds up and looking out at the parking lot, Russ spotted the van that Agent Williams told him about. Putting his arm around Naomi and pointing through the blinds, he said, "That van over there is a listening post set up by the FBI. You know I really don't think it's a good idea to drink that after taking the sedative the doc gave you."

Naomi pushed her hair back away from her face. "I need very much to take a shower, probably a cold shower. Would you check on the boys?"

"I will check on our boys. That Agent Williams said he is coming up here sometime this morning. That reminds me, I lifted your cell phone out of your purse. It's on the dresser. He said he would call before he came up. So don't take too long in the shower."

When Naomi came out of the shower in her robe with a towel wrapped around her head, Russ reached into his toiletries bag and took out a small bottle of mouthwash and handed it to his wife. "Make sure you brush your teeth and rinse."

Russ and Naomi were dressed, Naomi in dark slacks and a light pink blouse. Russ put on his faded jeans and a brown tee shirt. The boys were in shorts and sweatshirts sitting on the floor in front of their parents watching TV—or pretending to be watching the television—when there was a knock on the door. Russ opened the door and looked down to see Agent Asa

Williams, the sun reflecting off his snow white hair. "Agent, I thought you were going to call?"

"Mr. Gallagher, I did call, but my call went right to voice mail."

Russ picked up the cell phone and looked over at his wife. "Naomi, what does this mean? I pressed the button and your phone seems to be dead."

"It means I forgot to charge it."

Pushing his hair back, he said, "Agent, I am so sorry. Please come in. Boys, go over to your room." Sitting on the edge of the bed, Naomi looked over and motioned for Russ to pull the straight-back queen's chair over for the detective.

Pulling the straight-back chair away from the window, he said, "Please sit."

Agent Williams had a small recorder in his hand. "Mr. and Mrs. Gallagher, do you mind if I record our conversation?"

Russ shook his head. Naomi replied, "No."

Taking a breath and looking over at the Gallaghers, he lay the recorder on the arm of the straight-back chair he was sitting in. "First, let me assure you that as soon as the troopers called in an abducted child, roadblocks were set up and search parties were being formed. You gave a photo of your daughter to the trooper. He sent it out as soon as you gave it to him."

Naomi was having a problem sitting on the edge of the bed.

Asa continued. "The FBI resources that are available include special agents to assist in interviews, neighborhood canvassing, roadblocks, evidence response teams, and a computer forensics and response teams. Normally they take the lead. We are teamed as equals with the Louisiana State Police."

Agent Williams repeated many of the questions already asked. Naomi was asked several times during the interrogation if she could give a description of the person that knocked her out.

"You said you were digging through the diaper bag?"

"Yes."

"Before you were knocked out, what did you see?"

"I felt someone tugging at the diaper bag. I smelled dead fish, turned to look up and briefly saw what looked like a fair-skinned Mexican, with unkempt mousy brown short hair. I did notice yellowed teeth. Oh, yeah. I don't think I'll forget the smell of her breath. I don't know which was worse: my baby's dirty panties or the smell of that woman's breath."

Looking at Russ, he said, "What made you stop at this particular restaurant?"

"We were hungry, plus Jacquelyn was not the only one that needed cleaning up."

Pausing the recorder, the detective asked if he could get a drink of water. Russ put some of the leftover ice in glass and filled it with water, handing the glass to the detective.

Turning the recorder back on, he said, "You said she was not the only one that needed to get cleaned up?"

"Yeah, Anthony had a small accident. He said he had to go pee. I don't think we stopped soon enough. Then he said not here, please not here."

"Russ. Do you mind if I call you Russ?"

"No."

"Did you tell anyone that you would be or might be stopping at this particular restaurant?"

Russ was thinking the only thing missing was that table with the bare lightbulb above it. The agent was sipping water from the glass, which made Russ think how much he would like a Coke or just a cool glass of water. Several hours passed before Agent Asa Williams left.

"Boy, he didn't leave any time too soon. I really have to pee."

Naomi let out a sigh and then took a deep breath. "Don't take too long. I'm next."

Coming out of the restroom, he said, "Did you do whatever you had to do to get that phone working?"

Skipping to the bathroom, she said, "Yes, Russell, I recharged it."

He could feel eyes on his back. Turning he could see the boys staring at him. "Okay, boys, what is it?"

Denny spoke up, "Just wondering… Think we could get a hamburger or sompum?"

"Naomi, if we go across the street to the diner, do we have to check in with the people in the van?"

"They can always reach me on my phone. Plus we are only going across the street."

Just as the four of them were about to go out the door, Russ literally ran into Agent Williams, "Oops. Sorry 'bout that. We were just heading down to the restaurant. My kids are like those birds you see with their mouths open."

"I was just coming up to see if I could borrow a piece of clothing that Jackie recently wore, preferably one that hasn't been washed. We are sure our suspects were at Honey Island. I'd like to use Jackie's clothing to let the dogs get a sniff. The video I saw has a stamp date well before your child was abducted. I don't think they will find anything in that swamp."

"That place across the street puts out a good breakfast. I've heard that they have the best beignets in all of Louisiana." Scratching his short white hair, he added, "Yeah, you should still have time for breakfast." Looking over at Naomi's raised eyebrows, he explained, "Oh, beignet is like a donut, but I'm sure they are a lot more fattening, or so I've been told." Looking at Russ then at Naomi, he said, "I really don't think either of you have anything to worry about."

Anthony ran out the door and right into Agent Williams. "Sorry."

"Seems like me running into your family is becoming a habit."

Tugging on Russell's pant leg, he said, "But Daddy, you just got to listen to me."

Denny chimed in. "Yeah, Daddy, please listen to Anthony."

Traffic was light. Looking both ways, Russ gabbed with the boys and ran across the street. Naomi was trailing behind.

Entering the restaurant, Anthony was still trying to tell his dad about Jackie. "Dad, you just got to listen."

Denny put his hand on his brother's head. "Dad, please at least tell someone."

"I promise as soon as Agent Williams comes back I'll tell him what Anthony said."

There was a little crowd upon entering the restaurant. Russ had smack right into a wheelchair. In the wheelchair was perhaps the oldest man he had ever seen—even older than the old Bedouin sheep herder he met in the Syrian Desert. This man's face was sallow and covered with an incredible trace of wrinkles. His bony white knuckles that grasped the arms of the chair almost threatened to burst through the tissue-paper skin. Extreme age had shrunk and twisted his body into the shape of a comma. There was a large man with a belly that threatened to bust out of his bib overalls. With red swollen eyes, he bent over the wheelchair and whispered something in the old man's ear. Looking first at Russell and then at Naomi, he said, "This here is my paw-paw, Mr. Boudreaux. I'm Kyle Renee Boudreaux."

Mr. Boudreaux raised a shaky hand and covered Naomi's hand. The old man spoke, barely audible, and with the sound of the oxygen tank on the rear of the chair, asked, "Comment ça va?"

Kyle spoke up. "My paw-paw asks, how's it going."

"Well, sir, we have had better days. As a matter of fact I know I have had better weeks," replied Russ.

Putting slight pressure on Naomi's hand and looking up with the clearest blue eyes, Mr. Boudreaux whispered. "Listen to the boy."

CHAPTER 8

A twenty-one mile drive up to Crow Agency Montana should have taken half an hour, but with the blowing snow and icy winds, they had already been on the road for over an hour.

They found Hospital Drive. The hospital appeared dark. The snow in the parking lot was deep. "Melvin, I don't think anybody is here. Look, its dark at the hospital and I don't see any cars in the parking lot."

"It's a hospital, Darlene. There has got to be somebody here."

Jackie's fever was still high. She was starting to stiffen in Darlene's arms. They fought their way to the doors. Melvin pulled on the door but it didn't budge. Looking at Darlene and yelling, trying to be heard over the howling wind, he asked, "What do we do now?"

Just then out of the corner of Darlene's eye she spotted movement. A man with a thick lambskin coat pushed the doors open. "Come in. Get out of the cold." Once inside the heat hit Darlene, taking her breath away, "Please, my baby is sick."

Melvin Wright stared at the female desk clerk, waiting until she finished her telephone conversation. Her name was Karen, and she was very pretty. She was also having problems with the computer on her small desk.

The girl at the desk finally got off the phone and motioned for them to come up to the desk. "You do know we are not accepting patients. I can have our ER doctor look at her."

"Darlene, I had not thought of that."

Slowly getting up off the chairs in the lobby, she asked, "Thought of what, Melvin?"

"Computers. That all we need is for our names to pop up somewhere. Believe me, they are already looking for us."

"Melvin, the way she is banging on that computer, I don't think it's working."

"That may be, Darlene, but to get the kid in here, I'm going to have to show them my tribal identification. When that computer gets back up, we are in deep shit. She just said they are not taking patients."

"Well, Melvin, I don't think they are looking for me. I still have my tribal identification. Remember my last name is Prescott."

Although it did not look like anyone was at the hospital, Melvin thought it was one of the janitors that opened the doors for him. Wandering around the desk, he noticed that there was some activity in the back.

Karen, the pretty girl at the desk, picked up the phone. Melvin was sure she was going to sound some kind of alert. She actually pushed a button on the phone and said, "Could Nurse Running Deer come to the admitting desk?"

A square-shaped woman wearing her black hair in a single braid, in white slacks and white smock with a blue sweater, came into the lobby. Looking over at Darlene, she asked, "Is that the baby with a problem?" Motioning for Darlene to follow her, she said, "Follow me. The doctor is waiting for her."

Melvin couldn't help staring at the nurse. The only time Melvin remembered seeing a Crow woman in braids was at a powwow.

Calling after Darlene, he said, "I'll just wait here."

Nurse Running Deer looked back at him. "You can come. The doctor is on his way. We just need to get this little thing comfortable."

While Darlene watched Nurse Running Deer lift Jackie onto a gurney and motioned for her to follow, Melvin patted his shirt, looking for his cigarettes. Finding a partially crushed pack of smokes, he went out the entrance. Standing at the edge of the driveway, he sensed a presence of someone. There was a shadow at the corner of his eye. For a second it felt as if his heart would stop. The reflection of the entry light eliminated a bear of a man with a pink puckered scar on his left cheek. He was wearing a lambskin coat. As the man turned to face him, Melvin caught the sparkle of a badge. "Sorry. I know I shouldn't but I really needed a smoke."

Looking directly into Melvin's eyes, the man asked, "I haven't seen you before. Where are you from, brother?"

"Me. That is my woman and little girl got us a place down in Lodge Grass. The baby is pretty sick. That's why I drove up here. We only got a clinic down there and it ain't open at night."

Melvin noticed the tribal policeman's large, brown, scared, and callused hands as he pulled his gloves off. "I am Sam White Horse. We try to send a patrol down that way when we can. It's real hard on a night like this." Sam White Horse pulled the ear flaps up on his fleece-lined hat. Taking his hat off the light from the door, he caught the puckered pink scar on Sam's left cheek. The scare seemed to run from the deep laugh lines around his eye almost to his chin. Pulling his fleece hat off, Melvin noticed that the policeman was wearing his hair long. It came down almost to his waist. He turned to enter the hospital. Looking over his shoulder, he said, "You never told me your name."

Melvin called over to the tribal policeman. "I am Melvin, and I just need to get some of this smoke in my lungs. I'll be right behind you."

Sam White Horse pulled one of the folding chairs in front of Karen's small desk. Karen had her back turned to him, filing the recent admission forms. Smacking his snow-covered hat against his knee, he startled Karen, and she turned abruptly to see the policeman. "I am so sorry, Sam. You really have to start making some noise when you come in."

Scooting the chair closer to her desk, he said, "I did. Didn't you hear me smack my hat against my knee? Could I get a look at your most recent admission? By the way, I thought you weren't admitting patients."

"That is true, but the child that just came in will not make it to Billings. Nurse Running Deer says she needs to be stable before she can be transported."

Leafing through the thin file, he looked up at Karen. "Says here that a Jackie Prescott was admitted. It has Darlene Prescott as her guardian. I don't see a man's name?"

"No, the woman said that the child, Jackie Prescott, was actually her cousin's kid. She was just watching her while the cousin went away for a while."

Picking up the registration form and perusing the form, he looked for the child's name, date of birth, and address. "Thanks," he said, handing the file back to Karen. "What is the cousin's name?"

"Sam, I do not know. The little girl started going into convulsions. I called Kate to take her back. Never got a chance to finish the form."

"Something ain't right. That is a little white girl. I mean freckles and red hair?"

"Sam, my sister lives in Billings. She married a white, and two of her kids have a complexion like cream. I haven't seen them in a while, but I think the youngest has red hair."

Starting to get up, Sam stopped and turned back toward Karen. "Did you use the computer? I mean did you transmit that information to Public Health?"

"No, Sam, the computers are down. I thought I would get the rest of the information later."

Sam heard the static from his radio. "Sam, you there?"

"Yeah, boss, I am still here."

"Okay, wise guy. What is your twenty?"

"I am at the hospital thawing out. Got a bad feeling. There is a stranger here. Got a funny feeling about him. From what I can tell he and his woman brought in a little white girl."

"Well, if we ain't got any wants or warrants, just let it alone. Give me a name. As soon as the computer comes up, I'll check on your stranger. I am surprised the radios are working."

"I am going to grab some of that hot stale coffee they have here. Know what I just figured? Over."

"What is that, Sam?"

"Ya know the four-wheel drive on these SUVs ain't worth a healthy shit on this ice."

"Ten-four. Be careful out there."

Just as Sam was filling a paper cup with hot coffee, a middle-aged woman with unkempt mousy brown hair came running out of the ER, screaming and breathing as if she was having trouble catching her breath. "Aweee! There's a ghost in there. There's a ghost in there."

Darlene stopped in front of the bear called Sam. "Officer, there is a ghost in there."

Melvin was just inches behind Darlene. "Darlene, calm down." As Melvin tried to hold her, she shook him off her, like a dog shaking water off.

Sam came over to Melvin and Darlene. Darlene was completely incoherent. Melvin spoke up. "Officer, I don't know what that is about."

Nurse Kate Running Deer followed close behind, with a stuffed pink bunny in her hand. "Ma'am, that little girl is supposed to be in a sterile environment. I'm sorry, but you just can't leave"—she said, handing them the stuffed bunny—"this in the oxygen tent with her."

Sam tried to lightly touch Darlene. She shook his hand off her shoulder. Walking toward the entrance, she turned back to Melvin, "Melvin, I got to get out of here."

The policeman just stared at Darlene and Melvin. "Don't you want to be here with the little girl?"

Melvin spoke. "We are not going far. Darlene is just very tired. I am sure once she calms down she will be able to go back in there with the baby."

Nurse Running Deer had been standing off to the side. "Sam, it's okay. The little girl's fever has broken, and she is now sleeping. We have monitors on her. She is now being given antibiotics. She had to be intubated." Responding to Sam's unasked question, she said, "We are assisting her breathing. She is in an induced coma."

Melvin hesitated for a brief minute and then moved up to listen to the conversation. Looking up at the policeman, he said, "I'm sorry. Excuse me."

Answering Sam's unasked question, she explained, "Unlike the more typical way of being intubated or put on a breathing tube in their mouth, this child has the ventilator tube in her nose." She raised an eyebrow. "A ventilator is necessary for very young children. Poor thing has wires on her chest to monitor temperature and a probe to help regulate her temperature and probes to monitor her heart rate and respiratory or breathing rate. On top of that, there is an IV in her belly button. Plus, all this we need to keep her hydrated, so she is being given fluids. You know, Sam, if I hadn't been doing this for a very long time, after seeing my baby with all those tubes and needles, I would probably like to run out of here too, but then again I couldn't leave her, not for a second."

Melvin nodded toward the nurse. "I'm going to see how Darlene is doing. You know I'm sure she is concerned."

Looking at Melvin, "I understand the child is not yours?" asked Nurse Deer.

"That's true," Melvin replied. "Is she going to be all right? Is she gonna be all right?"

Starting to walk back toward the small cubicle where they had Jackie, she said, "Mr. Prescott, we will do all we can. She really is in bad shape. It is a good thing you got her in when you did. I don't suppose you have her health history or her shot records. You know the immunizations she may have had?"

Melvin was starting to sweat. "I'll check with Darlene."

Once outside Melvin came up behind Darlene and turned her toward him. "Listen, Darlene, we got to get out of here. That cop is asking a lot of questions."

"What about your friend Larry?"

"He's not gonna want the product now. He may want his money back. We'll take care of that whenever."

Climbing into the van, Melvin literally grabbed Darlene by her arms and pulled her into the van.

"Melvin, we just can't leave the baby here."

"Why not? She is being taken care of. Besides I don't think we are going to get the rest of our money anyway. I mean the package is damaged."

Looking back at the door to the hospital, he hoped that the policeman wasn't watching him. "You know, Darlene, Larry may not want her, but I know somebody who would pay a lot for a little girl like that."

"What are you saying?"

"I'm saying there are a lot of men out there that would pay a pretty penny for something so young and pretty."

"What are you saying, Melvin?"

Melvin just glared at her. "Darlene, we made a deal with a very dangerous man. That little girl was going someplace where they have a lot of little girls. Probably someplace in the Middle East."

"You mean she was going to be somebody's property?"

"Come on, Darlene. We need to get out of here. There's something weird about that cop."

Darlene slammed against the door of the van as it went fishtailing out of the parking lot. "Take it easy, Melvin. I just barely got the door shut."

Stepping out the front door of the hospital, Sam looked up to see a blue van fishtail out of the parking lot. He tried to get a look at the license plate, but it was dark and too far away. The one thing came to Sam's mind. *That has to be Melvin and his woman. Why are they leaving that baby?*

Clicking her seat belt, Darlene looked down to see a pink stuffed bunny ear sticking out of the bag she called her purse. "Melvin, we have to go back."

"What do you mean we have to go back?"

"I've got the baby's stuffed bunny. She'll want it when she wakes up."

With his hands tight on the steering wheel, he said, "Darlene, I was getting that feeling. I have a bad feeling. We need to get as far away as possible."

"Are we going back to our place?"

"Only for a few minutes. We need to get a few things then hit the road." Patting Darlene on her knee, he said, "We'll be at our place real soon. Just keep your eyes open. Let me know if you see anyone—cars, people, anything."

* * *

With wheels spinning and the van fishtailing, they finally pulled into their drive. Melvin did not turn the engine off right away. He didn't see anyone. Whatever tracks they had left earlier were covered by fresh snow. His heart felt as if it dropped to the pit of his stomach when he noticed the front door to the trailer was open, just slamming back and forth in the wind. The lights in the kitchen were on so he turned the light of the van off and coasted closer to the double-wide. "Darlene, did you lock the door?"

"I don't remember."

"What about the lights?"

"Melvin, I can't remember. We were in a hurry to get the kid to the hospital."

"Darlene, stay right here. Let me take a little look."

Creeping up on his own crib, he avoided the open door and snuck up to the kitchen window. The window was a little high even for him. He found an old plastic milk crate he had used to transport his extensive video collection. He stood on it and looked through the window. It seemed empty. He went around to the back window. There was no sign of activity. Brushing ice and snow off his trousers and pulling his gloves off, he went to the van. "Darlene, if somebody was here, they are gone now. You need to get your bag and pack some stuff you might need. I'll do the same."

* * *

The last of the stale coffee had worn off. Sam White Horse was trying to pull his gloves off so he could rub his eyes when static from his radio broke through his fugue. "That you, boss?"

"Yeah, Sam. What is your twenty?"

"Last patrol of the night. I wonder why it is so quiet out here. Think it might be the driving winds and the blowing snow?"

"Okay, Sam, don't be a smart-ass. Listen, the power is back and I got a fax here you might be interested in. I know you want to go home, but I really think you might be interested in what I got. I'll put a fresh pot on."

"Why not. This was the last section I was going to check on anyway. See you in a few."

Smacking his hat against the outside wall and stomping his boots on the mat outside the office, he announced, "Okay, Nathan, I'm here. What's up? I'm about to crash and burn right here."

Nathan Green was about sixty years old, with portions of his long braids gray streaked. His skin was a weathered brown, with deep laugh lines. He had a stomach that hid his belt buckle, while he stood and poured coffee in a deep ceramic cup with the name Sam on the side. Handing the cup to Sam and sitting behind an old splintered desk, he said, "Well, Sam, it seems everyone in three states is looking for a blue cargo van. Got pictures of the van with Montana tags outside a bait shop. Inside the shop the clerk had his throat slit. It is also possible that a Melvin Wright, the registered owner of the van, has abducted a little girl."

"Okay, Nate, why did you call me back here? Shouldn't I be tracking him down?"

"Sam, you told me he took off. No need to try and track in this weather. The little girl is still in the hospital. Right?"

"You got an address to go with that registration?"

"Yeah, but I think we need to try and get this little girl back with her parents."

"Well, Nathan, what do you want me to do."

"I'm calling Rides the Horse," he said, looking over at Sam, "to relieve you. You get back to the hospital make sure nobody tries to move that baby."

Sam went into the small locker room, threw cold water on his face, dug in his locker for a clean dry pair of socks, threw the damp socks on the bottom of the locker, and changed his shirt. Bundled up, he headed back for the SUV. Calling back to Nathan, he said, "Okay, Lieutenant, I'm heading back for the hospital."

By the time he got back to the parking lot, his SUV had a thick layer of snow covering it. *I can't believe this. I was sure the storm had let up.* The flakes were thick. By the time he got to the SUV, the wind was blowing and the snow was coming down sideways.

In the ICU, Sam pulled a folding chair outside the cubicle that Jackie was in. A doctor and Running Deer were in and out of the small cubicle. Sam thought he knew the doctors here and the few nurses that worked in the hospital. There seemed to be two doctors. The only reason he assumed they were doctors were the stethoscopes around their necks. He recognized one of the doctors but did not recall ever seeing the short dark one.

He had no idea how long it would take Robert Rides the Horse to relieve him. Time doesn't hold that much meaning for his Crow brother. He walked to the reception area, looking for the coffee pot. Karen was still sitting at her desk with her head over her computer. Looking up with a start, she said, "Sam, I told you about sneaking up on people."

"Sorry. Just waiting for Rides the Horse to relieve me. Say, I don't think I've ever seen this many medics here. This being a public health hospital and all, plus the last I heard this place is not a real hospital."

"There were doctors in earlier. Something about letting us be a hospital again. There was a couple doctors in from Billings. Got stuck by the storm. One doctor attempted to get to a motel. One doctor stayed here to help out with our one and only patient."

Turning her back toward Sam, she said, "Must be the storm. I've worked this shift for a while now, but for some reason I can barely keep my eyes open." Pouring coffee in her mug, then just staring at the coffee, she said, "I swear, Sam, if I even have another sip of this coffee, I'll be up for the next eight hours just running back and forth to the bathroom. Course, I could just go to sleep on the pot."

Wiping her eyes with her knuckles, Karen stretched and walked back over to her desk, stopping in front of it. "Sam, this may come as a surprise, but the coffee is fresh."

"That alone will keep me awake."

Pacing back and forth, then looking at Sam, she said, "Sandra is supposed to be my relief. Katie Woods, the admin supervisor, said she'd be in first thing in the morning. Don't really know what that means."

"Well, Karen, we may both be waiting. It doesn't look like this storm is going to stop any time soon."

CHAPTER 9

Naomi's phone rang at 4:30 in the morning. Naomi put her phone on speaker and woke Russell. It was Myra, Russell's mother. "Kids, I know you are going through a real black time. Have you heard anything about Jacquelyn?"

Russell picked up the phone and held it out so that Naomi could hear it. "They are telling us that they are sure Jackie is no longer in Louisiana."

"I really hate to tell you, but Dad is in the hospital. He went in for his normal check-up and it was decided that he would need to stay. The doctor told me that they need to get him ready." As he looked up at Naomi, his mother continued, "Sorry, your dad has a problem with the way I think too. They are expecting his lung and heart will be here by Friday. You know it's funny, he wasn't acting any different. The cough wasn't even that bad. The only thing different was that he hadn't had a cigarette all day. It was as if he knew they would be calling today. Listen, if you don't think you can make it, I'll understand."

Russell looked over at Naomi. She nodded her head. "Mom, we will be leaving here shortly. We are not going any place but Texas until we know what's going on with Dad."

The Gallaghers reluctantly checked out of the motel and at Agent Williams' suggestion bought a cellular phone. He gave the number to Agent Williams and after feeding the boys and three cups of coffee for both Naomi and him, they were once again on the road heading for Houston, Texas.

Russell asked. "Naomi, would you look for the turn-off to Deer Park?" Shaking his hands one at a time, he said, "Don't know why but staring at the side of the road looking for highway signs has me roaming all over the road. Good thing it's not rush hour."

"Russ, I think we are supposed to be looking for the Center Street exit."

Surprisingly, at least for Russ, he found himself in a driveway and his mother standing out on the front patio. "Okay, boys. You see that woman in front of that door?"

Denny piped up. "Oh, Dad, I know Grandma." Anthony chimed in. "Me too."

Before Russ had the car completely stopped and Naomi could say another word, the boys were out of the car.

"Hey, Myra, sorry, things aren't going to well for either of us."

With tears in her eyes, Myra said, "I just got back from the VA. Bryan says he feels about like he always does. You know, a little tightness in his chest. Says there doesn't seem to be any new pains. But you people have to be going through your own kind of hell. You know me and Dad have had our time, and I know that this time here on earth is only temporary." Looking at her son and grabbing Naomi's hand, she said, "But this baby has a whole life to look forward to. I've been bending our Good Lord's ear daily. I'm at the day chapel at the church. Sometimes three or four times in a day. If I'm not here, I'm at the chapel at the VA."

Naomi looked at Myra, "You know, Mom, I can't think of anyone else I'd rather have praying for me and Jackie than you. Don't get me wrong. I'll accept everybody's prayers. Believe me, our prayers with Bryan and you as well. You know we should be celebrating Russ made it home."

* * *

Asa was sitting at his desk across from Tom Walton. Even with the air-conditioner on and the ceiling fans turning, he had the knot on his tie pulled halfway down his open blue long-sleeved dress shirt with large sweat stains around the armpits, and his tropical weight suit jacket was hanging on the back of his chair. There was a time when he first started with the bureau that the only color shirt that was recognized was white, and agents were considered out of uniform without their suit jackets on. The red light on his desk phone started blinking, and then the old-fashioned ring. It startled him as since the advent of the cellular phone, the landlines were rarely heard, especially in Baton Rouge. Picking up the phone receiver, he answered, "Special Agent Williams."

"Is that you, Asa?"

"You got me, friend."

"Friend, is it? This is Nathan Green. Don't blame you for not recognizing me. What, it's been thirty years since we shared a hooch in 'Nam?"

With a brief hesitation, he scratched his head. "More like forty years. Chief? Where the hell you calling from?"

"It's lieutenant, Crow Tribal Police. You know I never did like being called Chief."

"Okay, Nathan, what have you got for me."

"I got your fax and the picture of the little girl, and I'm pretty sure we have your little girl up here. I haven't seen her yet, but one of my patrolmen identifies the picture you sent to us. She's in pretty bad shape, but I'm sure it's her and she is in the hospital here in Agency Montana. My officer Sam White Horse was there when she was checked in."

"Has she been molested?"

"I haven't had a chance to look at her, but I don't think she has been molested. She is being treated for double pneumonia. The bastard that brought her in has vamoosed. We'll keep an eye on her. Seems like the state of Montana is snowed in right now. The closest airfield is in Billings, and it has been closed and probably will be for a while."

"Nathan, the bureau has their own air force."

"Do your best, Asa. Be sure to bring your foul-weather gear."

"Nathan, that is amazing. Here in Baton Rouge we have the air-conditioner plus the ceiling fans running at full blast. Well, the fans may not be at full blast."

* * *

After waiting in line for fifteen minutes, he handed the keys to his car to a valet. Russ thought he was at the Veterans Administration Hospital. Myra pointed out that the sign above the door stated that they were entering The Michael E DeBakey VA Medical Center.

"Wow, you guys are really gong downtown," remarked Naomi.

Naomi, Myra, and Russ, with the two boys, headed into the VA. "Mom, are we going to get any flak bringing the boys in with us?" asked Russell.

"No, Russell, your boys are, or appear to be, well behaved. I'm sure it will be okay."

Russ stopped and looked down at his leg. He was feeling a vibration. Hearing music, other than what was coming over the VA speaker system, he said, "What?"

"Russell, that's your phone," Naomi remarked with a slight grin.

Stepping off to the side, he put the phone up to his ear. "Hello, hello?"

Naomi grabbed his phone. "Russ, tap the phone here."

"Mr. Gallagher, now I don't want you to get your hopes up, but I think we have located Jackie."

"I'll be there."

"Sir, I'm just keeping you up to date on what we are doing. Let me check this out first."

Naomi reached over Russell's shoulder and put the cell phone on speaker. "Special Agent Williams, this is Naomi. Where is my baby?"

"We think she may be in Montana. Tom and I will be flying up there as soon as the weather clears."

"Naomi again. It's 80 degrees outside. What's wrong with the weather?"

"I know Louisiana is hot and humid, but Billings, Montana, is below zero with blowing snow. Let me do my job. I'll call you as soon as I have anything."

Bryan Gallagher had a breathing tube in his nose. He was hooked up to an IV. There was a Kindle propped on his knees. Looking up, he said, "Hey, gang, are these two guys my grandsons?"

Russell spoke. "Yeah, Pop. It's been a while, but if you remember the little one with the—what do I call it—the platinum hair is Anthony, and this other guy is Dennis."

"Russell, I might be dying, but I am not feeble. It is true they have grown like weeds since the last time I saw them."

With his eyes starting to water, Russell remarked, "Are you really that anxious to leave us?"

"No, son, I'm not, but I am not about to tell myself stories. Listen, surgery, is still a possibility. Fact is, the reason I'm here now is for them to pump me up with antibiotics. They're expecting my new plumbing in by Friday. Now what is going on with that little girl of ours, Jacquelyn? Have you heard anything?"

"Yeah, Pop. The FBI agent called, telling me that he thinks he knows where she is."

Leaving the VA and Bryan in pretty good spirits, they headed back to Deer Park. Russell looked back at Naomi and then at his mother. "My God, how do you people handle this traffic?"

Giving Russell a playful punch on his shoulder, his mother said, "Well, son, I try to avoid it."

From the backseat Anthony was literally pounding on his father's shoulder. "Daddy, Daddy, please listen to me?"

Glancing back over his shoulder, Russell replied, "What is it, Anthony?"

"Daddy, Daddy, Jackie is in a plastic tent. She has a tube in her nose and there are bottles with rubes coming out of them into her arms. There is a big tube coming out of her chest."

With a breath. Russ glanced back at Naomi. "Naomi, are you hearing this?"

"Yes, Russ, I heard."

Just then Denny looked at his mom and reached up to touch his father. "Please, Mom, Dad, listen to Anthony?"

Naomi spoke up. "Boys, we are all upset, but please, this is nonsense. There is no way you could possibly know where your sister is."

Myra looked over at her son and then glanced back at Naomi with a look of discomfort. "What is this all about?"

"Well, Mom," Naomi replied, "Anthony thinks he knows where Jackie is, and Denny doesn't help. He also thinks that Anthony knows where she is. I really don't need this."

"Naomi, don't be too hard on your boys. You know they are also having to deal with losing their sister. Truthfully, Naomi, I cannot imagine what you are going through."

Leaning forward, she said, "Myra, you are going through your own hell, and now this?"

"Don't get me wrong. Bryan and I have been married for almost fifty years. This… what we are going through is all a part of life. Believe me, he has been a real pain at times, but if something happens, I still know I'll miss him."

Glancing to his right, Russ said, "Mom, the sign says the next three exits. Which one do I take?"

"Take the one that says Center."

Sitting in his father's recliner and kicking off his shoes, Russ said, "Naomi, would you come over here for a minute?"

Sitting on the couch next to Russell, she answered, "Okay. What's up?"

"Well, that call that came in on my cell while we were entering the VA?"

"Yeah?"

"That was Special Agent Williams. He says that they got a tip from the tribal police up in Montana. They think Jackie might be in the Public Health Service Hospital."

Rising from the couch and heading for the bedroom, she said, "Well, come on, what are you waiting for. My baby is in some strange hospital. We have to be with her."

Walking into the room, Myra was wiping her hands on a dish towel. "I hope you don't mind, but your boys are out back with a few boys from the neighborhood."

"No, Mom. I hope they know enough to stay close."

"I did tell them and asked if they would please stay in our yard."

"Naomi and I were just talking about the phone call I got while we were at the hospital. Special Agent Williams, that's the FBI agent that is in charge of finding our baby. Anyway, there has been a sighting of what they believe is Jackie. As soon as the weather clears, he's going to check it out." Looking over at his wife, he said, "Naomi wants to go up to Montana. That is where she was supposedly spotted. The agent asked that we stay here. He says he was just keeping us informed, and he would prefer us not come just yet, or at least until he is sure it is Jackie."

The house phone rang. The color in Myra's face was completely drained. Looking down at the caller ID, she answered, "Yes." Picking up the receiver and listening, she said, "Yes. This is Mrs. Gallagher." Gently placing the receiver back on the cradle, she announced, "That was the VA. They had hoped to schedule his surgery for the end of the week. Seems they just found a match. They are taking him in for surgery tonight."

Grabbing her purse, Naomi looked up to see Anthony and Dennis standing by the car. As Russell and Myra climbed into the car, "What is this?" she asked, looking at the boys.

Anthony replied, "We are going back to the hospital?"

Russell grabbed Anthony's shoulder. "Were you listening while Grandma was on the phone?"

With raised eyebrows, the boy answered, "No. Just knew."

CHAPTER 10

Looking in the refrigerator, Darlene said, "Melvin, somebody has been in our refrigerator."

"What?"

"I said somebody has been here since we were here a few hours ago."

With a bag half full, Melvin came out to the kitchen. Opening the refrigerator and looking in, he said, "There's no food in here, but that ain't unusual. How do you know that somebody's been here?"

"Well… there was pickles in the door. The jar is in the trash can. Any other food that was in there was starting to grow weird stuff on it, plus it stank, so I threw other stuff out when we were here before. I know I didn't throw out the pickles. They actually taste better when they been in there a while."

"Darlene, that is disgusting."

"It's just a little spooky."

"That's why we got to get out of here. Now get what you think you're going to need, and let's get out of here before they come back or the weather gets worse."

Climbing in the van, Melvin heard music. "I think your purse is playing music."

Digging in the bag she called a purse, Darlene pulled out her cell phone. "I don't understand. I didn't pay the bill, but the phone seems to be working just fine."

Throwing the bags into the van, Melvin pointed to the van. "Darlene, get in and buckle up. I'm just gonna check our crib out. You know, make sure all the lights are out, make sure we haven't forgotten anything."

Music again. Melvin stopped and turned back toward the van. "Is that the phone again?"

Digging it out of her bag once more, she answered, "Hello? This is Darlene. He's right here."

"What's up? That you, Larry?"

"Yes, my friend, this is Al-Abadi Labeeb. I am at the Public Health Hospital."

"How did you know your package was there?"

"Listen, Melvin, it was not that hard to figure it out. Were you just going to leave her here?"

"A tribal policeman was getting a little too curious."

"So you taking off will stop him from checking on you?"

"Probably not, but if I take off now, he may not be able to find me."

"Well, my friend, find a good place to hide. I will take care of our package."

Climbing back out of the van, he said, "I'm just going back in to make sure nothing is out of place."

A few minutes later, Melvin was back in the truck. "Darlene, did you leave the lid off the peanut butter? You also left a spoon in the jar."

"Melvin, I did not even look in the cupboard. I forgot we had peanut butter."

With his eyebrows raised, he turned to look at Darlene. "Okay. That's enough of that. Let's just get out of here."

"It must have been Larry."

Pulling out of his snow-crusted driveway, he said, "I think I know a place we can stay off the radar. There is a little town I know that is up in the mountains of Colorado. If anybody even thinks about us..." Darlene was just staring at him. "Well, they'll soon forget. They normally only search for kids and people like us for a few days. They just don't have the money or manpower to keep looking."

Looking over at Melvin, she asked, "What's the deal with this Larry guy?"

"We really need to get off the Rez. Well, I heard about this guy when I was at Angola. Larry gets online orders from all over the world. Very rich Arab or Sultan—whatever they call them—decides he needs to add another woman to his harem, or maybe they need somebody to do the cleaning or wash their dishes. He sends people like me, you and me to fill orders. In the meantime, he and his friends got to have their fun and when they are done, the product may be slightly used, will be shipped out to their destinations, some as far away as Bosnia and Thailand. Some may stay here in the States. There are a lot of rich whites, both men and women. They like having help around the house. Then there are the women that don't want to have a baby. It might just mess up their figure. Oh, they want a newborn. This is the first time to my knowledge that he has requested one of this age. I guess if they get them at four or five, they don't have to housetrain them."

Feeling the van slide, Melvin tightened his grip on the steering wheel. "Ya know, I've done business with Larry before. He normally wants girls and women from Indian reservations. You know, teenage girls that aren't far from working the streets. Especially one that have been kicked out of their homes. He always pays well, and the girls I pick up don't normally give me much hassle. They're hungry and cold and ready to get off the streets."

"But Melvin, why that little one? Why did we have to go to Louisiana? You told me when we met you never, never wanted to go back to Louisiana?"

"I wasn't sure I was gonna do this for him. But when we ran out of money… Anyway, he had been tracking this little one for a while. He gave me the numbers on the Florida tags. I mean, how hard could it be?"

Melvin turned off the main highway onto a farm-to-market road heading in the right direction that was not covered in snow and ice, or at least any ice he could see. The van was still skidding on the black ice he could not see.

* * *

Anthony was still in the trailer hiding in a closet in a room that didn't look like it was used much. He went back into the kitchen, found a spoon in a drawer, opened the jar of peanut butter, and took another spoonful. He had been to the hospital and gave Jackie her stuffed rabbit. He had to get back to the hospital. He felt something was wrong. Those bad people were not going back to the hospital. He had to get back to his sister.

He knew his sister was in a plastic tent in a hospital. He saw her. He put her bunny in the tent with her. What he didn't know was the name of the hospital. *Public Health? I guess that is as good a name as any. It's cold. This ain't Texas or Florida.*

There was a different lady at the desk. She looked up and saw him. "Hello, I'm Mrs. Woods. Are you here with your folks?"

"Yeah… Yes, ma'am. They went back to visit my brother."

"Who is your brother?"

What am I going to do now? Putting his hands up to his eyes and trying to snuffle and whimper like he was going to start to cry, he said, "They don't want me in there 'cause they say I might make him sicker."

It worked. She went back to the desk and picked up some kind of magazine

Managing to slide past a very big policeman with long black hair, he managed to get near Jackie's plastic tent. *There is a little dark man standing with other people in doctor clothes: long white doctor coats.* Anthony couldn't see his face. It was covered with a white mask, like what doctors wear. He did notice the little man's eyes. Anthony just knew he didn't look like the rest of the doctors. *Now I remember that is the man that was watching us at the airport.*

Mrs. Woods reminded Anthony of his grandma, but this lady was tan with brown eyes and a lot heavier than the other lady. The lady he was looking at had dark brown hair. *Grandma is white, most of the time, unless she has her cheeks painted red, plus her hair is mostly silver, and curly.*

Trying to get a closer look at his sister, one of the doctors, a tall skinny one, looked directly at him. "What are you doing back here, son?"

"Sir, that is my sister. How's she doing?"

"Where are your folks?"

"My mom needed to go home to get her medicine."

"Well, son, you need to go wait out front. Let me know when your folks get back."

Anthony didn't see Jackie's bunny. *I wonder if they throwed her bunny away.*

* * *

Robert Rides the Bear was sitting in a metal folding chair next to the desk occupied my Katie Wood. "Katie, I'm going to grab a cup that coffee and head back toward that baby. You got the duty today?"

"Actually Sandra was supposed to be here. Guess she's having trouble getting through the snow. I told Karen that she could crash here. I told her it was really hard to get through the blowing snow. She said she didn't live that far. She's supposed to call me when she gets home. I don't know what the bosses will say. You know, we are not supposed to admit patients. What are you doing here?"

"Seems like there is a young one, I mean really young, back there. Boss thinks she is a kidnap victim. I'm just going to grab this coffee and head back there. I relieved Sam a few minutes ago. Didn't take him much time to clear out of here."

Robert Rides the Horse was back at the coffee pot. There were a few people in the reception area, but nothing like most days, like when the winds were close to calm and the snow wasn't a foot deep. "Katie?"

Sliding her desk chair back and turning toward Robert a little abruptly, she asked, "What is it, Robert?"

"I'm sorry. Did I do something to upset you?"

"No, Robert. It's just days like today seem to bring the worse out of me. Plus I was supposed to be working on our accounts. You know, trying to figure out how we can take care of these people. Trying to figure out how we can get recertified so we can actually treat patients. I did hear from Sandra. Seems she is having a little trouble getting a babysitter. Normally her kids would be in school. No school today."

Just then Robert's radio squelched. "Robert..."—static—"Robert, can you hear me?"

"You're weak."

"If the landline is…"—screech… static… "call dispatch."

"Will do."

"Say again. Did you copy?"

Picking up the receiver on the desk next to Katie, he said, "Yes, dispatch. Got a message to call you."

"Stand by. The captain is getting on the line."

Scratching his head, Robert answered the captain. "What can I do for you, Cap?"

"How is the little girl doing?"

"I was just in there. She seems to be sleeping, although she has tubes coming out of her little body, and there are more doctors here than I have ever seen. Didn't know we had that many doctors. I thought they stayed in the big city where they actually got paid."

"Robert, don't let anybody take her any place. She is apparently a kidnapping victim. As soon as they can fly into Billings, the feds will be here."

"Captain, I'm sitting right outside the little cubicle." The lone bed was positioned near the opening in the curtains around the cubicle, surrounded by IV racks, medical sensors, and several pieces of equipment. There were hoses, cables, and clear plastic tubing.

Hanging up the phone, Roberta said, "Katie, I guess it's just the two of us?"

"Not for long. While you were on that line, I got a call from Sandra. Seems they sent her husband home from work, so he is going to watch the kids." Looking up over half-lens reading glasses, she said, "It's not that you're not good company, but you need to be in there and I need to get a lot of paperwork done. This is the perfect day. Unless we get a ten-car pile-up, I don't see very much business."

* * *

Sam made it through the weekend. He had been spending twelve hours at the hospital. It was 8:02 AM when Robert showed up to relieve Sam. "Give me a few minutes, Sam. I need to use the head."

"Robert, I know the Crow have a reputation of not letting time get in our way, but brother, this staying in one spot is about to drive me up the walls. I've been pacing since four this morning, and if I even smell another cup of coffee, well, you know the rest of it."

Robert was still pulling his trousers up as he came out of the restroom. "I am sorry, Sam. Listen, I'll be early tonight. I promise."

"Say… Robert, I stepped outside a few minutes ago, and guess what—I could see the mountains, and there was a strange light in the sky. Karen told me they call that the sun."

"Okay, Sam. Just let me get something to eat and a few hours' sleep. Oh yeah, the feds should be here tomorrow."

Sam sat in the hard metal folding chair, stretching his long legs, finally getting up off the chair and pacing. Looking in on Jackie, he noticed that the tube in her chest had been removed. She still had a tube in each nostril and an IV needle in her foot. There was that strange doctor left in the little cubicle—a short dark man with what appeared to be dark stubble. He recognized the other doctor, but there was something about this one.

Taking a deep breath in the frosty evening, he looked up at a full moon—the first time he'd seen the moon in days. He thought about sitting in his warm trailer with a cold beer. There had to be something on the tube. Just then he saw the dark little doctor. He had to ask, "Doctor, Doctor."

The little man, whose face appeared to have a three-day growth of dark whiskers, stopped and turned toward Sam. "Were you talking to me?"

"Yes. I haven't seen you around here before."

"Oh, I'm Doctor Abadi. I'm a pulmonary specialist from Helena. I was down here to evaluate the Public Health Hospital. I got stranded by the blizzard. That little girl in there was in pretty bad shape, so I offered my assistance." Heading back toward Jackie, he said, "I understand that this is not a real hospital."

Calling after the doctor, Sam answered, "This was a hospital up to a few months ago. The only hospital available for the people here and as far south as Lodge Grass."

The waiting room was starting to fill up. Looked like everyone was waiting for the snow to stop and the roads to be plowed. Sam took one more deep breath and squinted against the red sun setting behind a snow white mountain that appeared to be reaching for a rapidly changing sky from an azure to indigo.

Coming back inside, he rubbed his hands together, making a fist and blowing into each hand. Most everyone had left. There was one nurse in with the child, a doctor in the ER, and a nurse practitioner. Nurse Running Deer, one of the two nurses on staff that was covering the night shift, stood directly in front of Sam as he came in the door. "I see you're here looking out for our little girl."

Taking off his coat and putting it on the back of the metal folding chair, he said, "Yeah. You know, don't you, that everybody has to be someplace. By the way, what do you know about that"—he said, pointing to the little man that looked like he needed a shave—"doctor over there?"

"I've never seen him before. I guess he is here from medical board. It is curious. You know, once the storm lets up the other visitor were out of here so fast all I saw was a flash. Does he bother you, Sam?" Turning to the cubicle, she said, "You know, with that doctor from Helena, we might not get in trouble for having an in-patient."

"It's probably just my paranoia, but there's something about him that bothers me. How about you? You the only nurse on tonight?"

"No, we'll have another nurse. The x-ray tech checked in." Running Deer was the head nurse and it seemed to Sam that she was fully in charge. One of the problems this little medical facility had was the lack of nurses. Most registered nurse went into Billings where the pay was slightly better.

Another doctor arrived. The waiting room was emptying rapidly. They were mainly dealing with minor injuries, a couple of bellyaches. Walking outside and seeing a full moon, Sam was not surprised when women in labor started coming in. It didn't surprise Running Deer, either. She anticipated this and had scheduled the appropriate nurses.

Sam was still squirming in the hard, uncomfortable chair. He did notice the full moon and was not surprised to see women obviously in labor coming in. Standing and stretching his long legs, he became aware that the last time he had seen Dr. Abadi, he was leaning over Jackie. He looked in the cubicle and the child seemed to be sleeping, only the IV line was left. He looked for the doctor. The little dark doctor was nowhere to be seen. Thinking to himself, *He probably finally took a break. Might have even gone back to his hotel, motel, or wherever?*

Not that the passing of time was ever of great concern to Sam, but this night he was anxious for his relief. Robert did come in early, if a person were to call thirty minutes early. Sam rarely if ever experienced resentment or envy, but looking at a well-rested, clean-faced Robert made him think of an earlier time when he felt he didn't need rest or sleep. Standing up as Robert entered, he said, "Good morning, Sunka Wakan."

"Sam, do I really look Lakota?"

"You know what the whites say? We all look alike."

"Anyway, I had a very good night."

"Ah… you had a date. Not to worry, the feds should be here today, and our little girl seems to be recovering."

CHAPTER 11

An agent from the Helena field office was waiting for Agent Asa Williams. Looking up with his hand out was a tall lanky blond-haired man wearing a charcoal top coat and a fur cap. "You must be Special Agent Asa Williams," he said, looking over at Tom, "and this must be the Agent Tom Walton I keep hearing about. I'm Agent Al Reed, out of the Helena field office. I would have thought you would be using the Bureau Lear jet?"

"I guess neither one of us are high enough on the list for that, although they said when I'm ready to go home, they would send one for..."—pulling out a handkerchief and wiping his nose—"what was that comment of the agent?"

"Our car is outside. Do you guys have any other luggage?"

"No. Just my carry-on."

Stepping outside the terminal, Asa remarked, "I can see why you're wearing a top coat. How far to Crow Agency?"

"Not far, 'bout fifty miles. The roads have finally been plowed. Do you need a cup of coffee or maybe something to eat?"

"No, I'm fine. I would just like to see that little girl."

Sitting in the right seat with Tom in the backseat of the sedan, Asa scratched at his chin. "Man, I have one dozy of a headache," he said, putting his head back on the headrest. Rubbing his throbbing temples, he said, "And before you say anything, it is not a hangover."

Asa couldn't help but notice the mountain. Looking out at the pale blue sky, he said, "You know, Reed, I know now why they call this Big Sky Country. It is truly amazing."

"Yes, it is, sir. I didn't think I'd like this assignment, but now if I were to get another assignment, I don't think my wife and kids will come with me. By the way, we are being followed."

Reaching up and turning the rearview mirror, he said, "You're right. Is that a maroon Chevy? Tom, Tom, take a look behind us."

Trying to re-adjust the rearview mirror, he said, "Do you know this guy?"

"First, stop calling me sir. It makes me feel old—I mean older. Damn, I'm pretty sure that is our victim's father. By the way, just don't call me sir when we are out of the office."

"Yes, sir. I mean yes."

Scrubbing a hand over his face, Asa asked, "Reed, find a place to pull over. I told these people to wait until I could confirm that we did in fact have their daughter."

Tom Walton leaned up against the front seat. Tapping Al Reed on the shoulder, "Is there going to be other agents at the hospital?"

Pulling on the shoulder of the road, he turned to look at Reed. "The Helena office is not that big, but there will be a few more agents there. You know we have to be nice, nice to the tribal police. There were very helpful and the police superintendent said he would be able to spare a few of his patrolmen."

Tom commented, sarcastically, "That was mighty considerate of him."

Agent Al Reed turned to Tom. "We have a very good relationship with the tribal police. It is true it has taken a while to gain their trust. When they heard that the little girl that they have in the Public Health Service Hospital might be a kidnap victim, the tribal police were more than willing to help."

The agents had stopped on the shoulder, and within a minute the Chevy pulled in behind them. Asa climbed out of the sedan. Breathing deeply, Asa tapped on the window of the Chevy. After the window was rolled down, he said, "Mr. Gallagher, just what are you doing?"

Looking up at Asa, he said, "That is my child and we have a right to be here."

Abruptly, at first, then with another breath and letting it out slowly, and deliberately calming and softening his voice, he said, "Mr. Gallagher… Russell. We don't know what we will be dealing with. If the person or people that took you child is here, this whole situation may get out of hand. I am concerned about Jackie's safety, and now I have to be concerned about your safety. I have to say this, you being here might very well cost us by either allowing the suspects to get away or endangering your daughter. And by the way, did you have to bring your entire family. Whatever happens, you people are going to make this whole procedure much, much harder."

"I'm sorry, and we will stay out of your way. But if that is Jackie in that hospital, she is going to want to be with her mother."

"Russell, you're right, but I cannot have you anywhere near that hospital. If your child is in there, I will call you as soon as I know it is safe. Just stay close."

Agent Reed turned to Asa. "There is a café not far outside Crow Agency. Why don't the Gallaghers stop in at the little café and wait for us? They'll be close enough that it will only take minutes for them to get to the hospital."

Asa looked over at Al Reed and then at Russell. "What do you think?"

Russell considered then stared back at his car and then Naomi. "That sounds like a good idea."

Walking back to the government sedan, Asa inquired, "Where is this café you're talking about?"

"It's not far from the hospital. It's just a little farther on I-90."

"Russell, you people follow us. We'll signal to you at the café."

No more than ten minutes passed when the government car signaled for Russ and his family to turn into the café parking.

The parking lot was fairly crowded for early afternoon. Russell was looking for a spot close enough yet also in a place where, if needed, he could get on the highway. There was a rusted blue van at the edge of the parking lot not far from the highway. Out of the backseat, Anthony screamed, "Daddy, Mommy! Over there!"

Naomi turned to look back at Anthony. "What, Anthony? What are you screaming about?"

"Look. Near the highway."

Just then there was an amplified sound like fingernails scraping across a chalkboard. "Russell! Pull over near that van."

"Naomi. Use your cell phone and call Agent Williams."

"Already done. He's on his way back here. The car is on the way back. He'll just get out here and his partner will go on to the hospital."

For Russ and Naomi, waiting for Agent Williams seemed to be taking forever. Every time Russ was looking at his watch every minute. One minute seemed like an hour.

From the backseat, Denny literally punched his father's shoulder. "Dad, look," he said, pointing to the van. "They're getting away."

With that Naomi pushed the door open and jumped out, running toward the van and then seeing the woman with the mousy brown hair, she screamed, "Oh no, you don't." As Naomi came up on the woman, the smell of the woman just about took her breath. She thought, *I'll never forget that putrid smell.*

Falling out of the car, Russell shouted, "Naomi, no! Come back here."

The man yelled. "Darlene, look out!"

By then Naomi had a handful of that mousy brown hair. "No, you don't. You are going to give me back my baby."

"Aaaa! Get off me. Melvin, help me."

Melvin started to grab Naomi as Russell came up and put his arm around the much bigger man's neck. Melvin tried to turn but found this much smaller wiry man hard to get away from. Russell squeezed tighter and tighter on the man's throat with his forearm. Melvin tried to turn into Russell's elbow, but was finding the hold that Russell had on him impossible to break loose. Melvin saw gray and then black. Russ felt Melvin go limp and let go, watching as Melvin collapsed to the ground. Naomi made a fist and putting her whole body into her punch, she felt bone and mush as she looked to see Darlene's smashed nose. With her hand up to her nose, Darlene fell unconscious to the ground. Naomi was about to jump on top of her. She could see herself killing this woman, the one that smelled like bad fish. There was no mistaking that this is the woman that knocked **her,** Naomi, out and took her baby.

"Anthony, do you hear that?" asked Denny.

"Sounds like a siren of a police car. I guess the blue and red lights are from the police too," commented Anthony.

The government car with Agent Williams stopped and Asa jumped as the car sped off. He rubbed his knees and thought, *I really do have to retire; that hurt.* Running or a close facsimile of a run, Agent Williams got up to the state patrol car, out of breath and reaching for his identification as the trooper reached for his side arm. Grasping for breath, he managed to get out. "Wait. FBI.

While the trooper took the FBI credentials out of Asa's hand, Melvin grabbed Darlene by her hair and managed to wake her. They both staggered to the van. With dirt, gravel, and a cloud of dust, they fishtailed onto the still-slick highway.

Bending over and trying to catch his breath, just trying to breathe, Williams stood up. He reached out with a shaky hand and grabbed his ID back and looked as the van disappeared down the highway. "Shit!"

With a very dumb expression, the trooper looked at Asa. "Is there a problem, Agent?"

Staring directly into the trooper's eyes, Asa said, "No, trooper, no problem other than you allowing our suspects to get away."

"When I rolled up, they appeared to be the victims, and that," he said, pointing to Naomi, "would have killed her if I didn't restrain her."

"Would that have been so bad?"

"I was sworn to enforce the law, and the two of them, both him and the woman, were about to kill someone."

"Trooper, let me ask you a question."

The trooper just gave Williams a defiant look.

"Trooper… Before you go out on patrol, or at the start of your shift—don't answer. Just listen. Do you guys get together for a briefing? You know, a little meeting. To see if there just might be something to look for while cruising these highways. Well, if you had, you would have seen or been told of a pair of murderers and kidnappers we have warrants on. Oh, if you didn't notice, every police agency has pictures of the couple we are looking for and that blue van. It is believed that the man you just released has killed at least one police officer, and probably more than a few civilians. Williams was evidently still out of breath. He just motioned to the trooper as if he were shooing a fly away. The trooper wasted no time in getting in his cruiser and departing. Agent Asa Williams barely staggered toward the Gallaghers' car. Naomi stepped out of the car and left the door open. Grabbing onto the roof of the Caprice, Asa almost fell, but did manage to plop on the seat.

Naomi noticed that Asa's complexion went from almost purple to a very pale white. Motioning for Russ to come and help her, she said, "Agent Williams, are you all right?"

Taking a breath and holding his chest, Asa reached into his breast pocket. "I don't suppose you got any aspirin in this car?"

Denny spoke up. "Mom, there is aspirin in the first-aid kit. It's in the glove box."

Handing Asa the aspirin and a bottle of water, Naomi asked, "Should I call an ambulance?"

"Thanks. I'm tempted, but I do feel better and we have to get your baby."

Russ looked at the agent. "Listen. Don't you dare drop dead on us?"

Taking a deep breathing and letting it out slowly, Asa looked up at Naomi and then at Russ and the boys. "Thank you. This has happened before. I normally have nitroglycerin in my pocket. The nitro must have fallen out of my pocket when I was running. I would appreciate it if you didn't mention this to my partner. I've got less than a year to go for retirement. Plus, as soon as I get back to Louisiana, I make it a point to see my doctor."

CHAPTER 12

Pulling into the parking lot of the Public Health Service Hospital, Sam couldn't help but look toward the mountain range and the setting sun. It looked to him as if once again business was as usual. Walking into the emergency room, he could smell the familiar odor of alcohol, antiseptic, an assortment of body fluids, and the all-too-recognizable smell of blood with the underlying stench of old pennies. The orderlies and the staff did an excellent job of keeping the area clean, but Sam always had an acute sense of smell.

Robert was seated at the admittance cubicle talking with Sandra. Walking over to Robert and interrupting what appeared to be a very animated conversation, Sam asked, "How's our little girl today?"

"The last time I looked in on her she was sleeping. Looks like all the tubes and monitors have been removed. She woke up a while ago crying, wanting her momma, but the doctor gave her a sedative, and she has been sleeping ever since."

"I thought we agreed to stay in that chair, by her cubicle? Well, let's go back and check on her?"

As he turned to go back to where the child had been sleeping, he saw Running Deer coming out. "Evening, Sam."

"Running Deer. How's our little girl doing?"

"Just came on shift. I'm heading back that way now."

They were at the cubicle in less than a minute. Looking over at the day nurse, they asked, "How's our little girl doing?"

The nurse looking a bit bewildered and raised an eyebrow. "There are no children in here. I did notice a child when I came on, but since we are not supposed to accept patients, I assumed she was to be transported to Billings."

Running Deer felt a catch in her chest and put her hand on her breast. "Who authorized her move?"

"There was a short Mideast-looking doctor standing by her bed." Running Deer was getting tense; the color in her face became chalky. "Do you have any paperwork on a Jackie Prescott?"

The nurse went to the nurse's station and looked through the paperwork. It seemed like it was taking a long time. She went through the paperwork twice. "Nothing."

Sam and Running Deer were now running to the cubicle where she was last seen. Sam looked where he saw her last. There was an old man lying on the thin examining bed, the one that had been Jackie's. Turning to the nurse, they asked, "There has to be paperwork on this child."

"No, sir, the last thing I saw was one of the visiting doctors hovering over her bed. When I came back, I was informed that the bedding needed to be changed."

Running Deer spoke up, and as calmly as she could, she asked, "Okay. How long has it been?"

The nurse was now beginning to sweat, even though the air-conditioning had the clinic feeling like a meat locker. Looking over at Running Deer, one of them asked, "I suppose it's too late to call a code yellow?"

* * *

Agents Reed and Walton had just arrived at reception. Walton spoke to the receptionist. "We're here to see a patient. A little three-year-old, Jackie."

The receptionist raised her head, then looked down at what appeared to be some kind of roster. "What's the child's last name?"

Tom Walton looked at the receptionist, "I don't know, but you can't possibly have that many three-year-olds in the ICU."

"Well, sir, first, we do not have an ICU. I don't see any Jackie on our roster."

At that moment there was a loud screech, followed by static, then the PHS's speaker system sounded an alarm, then the announcement that a code yellow was in progress.

Agent Reed walked over to the receptionist and calmly asked, "What is a code yellow?"

"Oh, one of our patients—not that we have in-patients—has probably wondered off. It happens a lot with some of our older patients."

The people at Crow Agency were used to seeing a tribal police cruiser, but rarely saw a cruiser with the sheriff's marking on it. The state police markings on the cruisers that were parked near the entrance to the clinic were even less likely to be seen.

Karen had just sat down at her desk. What she heard sounded like a herd of wild horses. She looked up to see men in police uniforms and two men wearing suits. One had on a tan top coat; the other man had a blue top coat draped over his arm. Both top coats looked more like heavily lined trench coats. Out of habit, she looked down at their shoes. She thought, *Nobody in these parts wear shoes like that. There is absolutely no way to keep a high-gloss shine on shoes in this part of Big Sky Country.*

Standing over the receptionist desk and looking down at Karen, one of them asked, "Where is the Gallagher child?"

Pushing her chair back away from the desk, she answered, "Agents, I just arrived here, but it seems that the child that I had been calling Jackie Prescott has been transferred to the hospital at Billings."

Agent Tom Walton moved Agent Al Reed out of the way and stepped forward. "Who authorized the transfer?"

"Sir, I can't find any paperwork on the child."

"There was supposed to be a police officer next to the child. Where was the police officer?"

"Like I said, I just came on shift. I don't know, but I'm sure that if he was supposed to be stationed next to the child, he was. There must have been a doctor or other person in charge that authorized the transfer. I'm sure it was a medical emergency."

"Don't parents or guardians have to be not only notified but give permission?"

"When the woman claiming to be her guardian ran out of here, she became a ward of the state. Oh, we made several attempts to contact her, but nothing."

"Surely you have paperwork authorizing Child Protective Services guardianship of a sick child?" asked Agent Walton.

Karen had just taken off her lambskin jacket and was about to put it back on, as she was feeling cold. Looking up at the FBI agents, she started to sweat and no longer felt the need for her jacket. She went through the paperwork on her disordered desk, then rifled through the filing cabinet.

She found what she was looking for. "Agents, it appears Child Protective Services never really came here."

Tom spoke up. "What do you mean they never came?"

"The blizzard was once again howling, and there was no way a social worker could get here." Raising her hand to quiet the FBI agents, she said, "I do have verbal authorization, with a file number. There was supposed to be someone here today to check in on the child."

Al Reed spoke up. "Did Child Protective Services take the child?"

Karen's eyes were starting to water. "No, sir. I have no paperwork indicating that she was removed by Child Protective Services. I will phone them right now."

* * *

Agent Asa Williams and the Gallaghers walked through the doors. Agent Williams went over to his partner. Naomi just stood still as if she was stationary, staring at the commotion in front of her. Anthony was yelling something. His brother Denny's eyes were red and tears were flowing. Russell was trying to console both boys. Holding his boys close and reaching for his wife, Russ asked, "What is happening here?"

Asa Williams motioned for the Gallaghers to come closer. "I am so sorry."

Naomi had no more tears to shed. Her voice was weak and raspy. "Why are you sorry, agent? Is my child alive?"

"Yes, she is alive, and her health is much better." Gazing outside the door and then looking at the Gallaghers, he said, "The people here think she may have been taken to a hospital in Billings. We have someone checking with the hospitals in Billings right now."

The reception area of PHS was starting to thin out. Most of the law enforcement officers had departed. There were a few people waiting to be seen. There was only one doctor and he specialized in emergency medicine. The nurses available were pediatric nurses and spent most of their time with the women in labor pains. Nurse Running Deer was doing the best she could in assisting the doctor.

Standing over the reception desk, Agent Tom Walton asked, "Karen. Your name is Karen?" He got her attention. "So this is not a hospital?"

"It used to be, but because of funding and the lack of qualified nurses, we are not supposed to operate as a hospital. The doctors—right now, there are three doctors—are well qualified, and with one exception, the registered nurses are more familiar with pediatrics and maternity."

Scratching his head, he said, "So what is your function here?"

"My function is to act as a receptionist. We can still act as a clinic, but most of our patients are here to have babies. We do care for the occasional emergency."

"One more thing. How did our little girl, Jackie Gallagher, wind up here?" asked Agent Walton.

"A man and a woman came in here. They said they were from Lodge Grass. Their clinic turns into a first-aid station and fire department at night. The man and woman claimed to be the little girl's guardians."

Denny noticed the policeman with his hair in braids standing near the entry to the little clinic. Turning to his brother, he asked, "Anthony, do you see that Indian standing"—pointing to a tall brown-skinned man the far side of the room—"over there?"

"I see him."

"Well, is he a policeman or an Indian?"

"Denny, we are on an Indian reservation, and yes, he is a policeman and an Indian."

Asa Williams went over to the Gallaghers. "Russell, Naomi, from what I could find out, your daughter is recovering from pneumonia. She is no longer critical. We have checked with all the hospitals in the area. We will check all the hospitals in the state and beyond. What I would really like you to do is go home and take care of the rest of your family. I promise that as soon as we find out anything, I will be in contact with you. Let me know where you will be. I know you had been staying in Houston. When you go back to St. Pete, call me."

Walking out with the Gallaghers to their car, Asa Williams bent down to the open passenger window. "I promise I will not stop until we find your baby."

Naomi looked up at Agent Williams. "Why here? What reason would they have to bring my baby here?"

"Naomi, I really don't know how to answer that. I guess it might have been random, but my friend Nathan—he is a lieutenant on the tribal police—tells me that there has been several Indian women missing. The bureau has been investigating with the tribal police for missing young girls and women, mostly teenagers looking for a way out of poverty. In general, accurate statistics on human trafficking victims are difficult to nail down because many women who manage to return are shamed into not reporting it. But I can tell you that in Northeastern Montana, we have definitely seen an increase in Native women who have been trafficked—an increase of 12 to 15 percent in the last year. They normally range in age from 15 years old to their early 20s. I've seen reports that some of the women were as old as 50. Taking babies is brand new." Turning away from the car, he added, "Just one other thing. I don't think whoever did this was planning on keeping her here in Montana."

Walking away from the Gallaghers, Asa turned, "I am sorry, that was very unprofessional of me. I know that did nothing to help you. I think it was probably for my benefit to hear myself say it. We will get Jackie back."

CHAPTER 13

The trip back to Houston was uneventful and very quiet. The boys barely spoke. Russell was driving and placed his hand on Naomi's knee. "Naomi, I'm at a loss. I don't know what to do next," Russell said.

"Russ, when we left Houston your dad was about go home. He is your father and we really need to check in on him. I've spoken to Myra. She says he seems to be recovering well. That he was told to exercise, but not to overdo it."

"You know, my dad doesn't know how to not overdo it. When he drinks, he has to drink more than anyone else. And you know how he smoked. Some people might say my dad has an addictive personality." Putting both hands on the steering wheel, he pulled down the car's sun visor and squinted into the sun. "But you are right, we do need to check in with the folks before we head back to Tampa Bay."

Naomi reached up next to her visor, removed her sunglasses, and handed the visor to Russ while she put her sunglasses on. "Do we go home and back to work, continue with our lives like nothing has changed?"

"Of course not. We try to focus on living our lives. I will never give up looking for our daughter. Going back to work and trying to focus will be the hardest thing I will ever do."

Naomi turned to look back at the boys. "You guys are awful quiet back there. What's going on?"

Denny leaned up against the front seat. "I know I used to complain about my baby sister, but you know I miss her, and I don't know if I'll ever be able to act as if everything is normal."

Denny and his mother both looked over at Anthony. Anthony was just staring out the window. Naomi called, "Anthony." Louder, this time, "Anthony!" and looked directly at Denny. "Denny, shake your brother." Still nothing. No movement, nothing. "Is he breathing?"

"Yes, Mom, he is breathing," he said, putting his hand on his brother's cheek and trying to turn Anthony's head. With some difficulty, he managed to slightly turn his brother's head. "But his eyes are open. It's like he is in a deep sleep."

Russ glanced over at his wife. "What's going on?"

"I don't know what is going on with your son," Naomi said.

"Something wrong with Denny?"

"No, your other son—you know, the white one," replied Naomi.

"Naomi, that is not even funny."

"Denny, is he hot or cold?"

"No, Mom. He's just sleeping, sitting up with his eyes open."

"Have you ever seen him do this before?"

"Yes, ma'am. The other night in the motel room I got up to go to the bafroom, and he just sat straight up with his eyes open. I tried to talk to him, but he didn't answer."

"Denny, sweetie, just keep an eye on your brother, and let me know if he starts breathing funny, or anything else that might be different."

"Okay. You do know my brother is just a little weird."

Letting out a breath, she said, "I don't really want to hear that. Although I do sometimes wonder about your brother."

* * *

It was warm and muggy. Anthony found himself standing in front of what looked like some kind of factory, no, not a factory. Maybe a warehouse. There was a very high chain-link fence around a large cement block building with large garage doors. He walked around the fence and on the other side of the building, there was an open gate. Down from the gate was an ocean, or that is what Anthony thought at first, but on a longer look, the waves on the shore were not crashing; they were more like lapping. Anthony knew this was no ocean but a very large lake. He once again walked around the building, but this time in the opposite direction. At a distance from the building was a black road. He saw a sign. From what he could make out, it was some kind of hospital, but it didn't say hospital. It said Women's Health Clinic.

He had to get inside that big building, whatever it was. He walked around the big building again. The big gates in the back near the lake were open. Once he got next to the building, he tried to peek in the windows, but they were too high. He found two metal milk crates. He knew it was a milk crate because he had seen them in the back of the school cafeteria. He put the crates by the window and climbed up. The window was real dirty and he couldn't see inside. He found himself standing in a very large room. The room looked like a big basketball court. He heard the sound of children, some crying, some screaming. At first he thought someone might spot him, but with the screaming children, that probably would not happen.

On the side farthest away from him, there was a counter and a lady in white nurse's clothes behind a counter. There was a window at the counter that the lady opened when she would call somebody. There was another room closer to where he was standing. Looking inside, he saw children. They all seemed to be little children, maybe four- and five-year-olds. Getting as close to the wall as he could, he then stood so close to the wall that he felt he was part of the wall. There were cots and beds in the room. He thought he spotted Jackie.

She was just lying on a lumpy mattress with dirty yellowed sheets. Her eyes were open and he was sure she spotted him. She had her thumb in her mouth and two of her fingers in her nose. She could move her arms and hands, but the rest of her body was tied to the dirty bed. She tried to get up, but the straps kept her on the bed. The clothes she had on looked dirty and wet. The clothing that the others were wearing were also dirty.

* * *

Anthony's eyes popped open. He turned to Denny. "What are you doing, Denny?"

"Anthony, you was sleepen' with your eyes open. Scared Mom, but I seen you do that before."

"Listen, Denny, Jackie is in a big warehouse, or maybe a hospital, with a bunch of other kids. I think they are getting to do sumthin' to Jackie and maybe the other kids. Mom and Dad won't listen to me. Somehow we got to get somebody to listen."

"Anthony, I told them you knew, but they ain't gonna listen to me either."

Russell tapped Naomi on the arm. "I'm getting tired. You want to stop for the night?"

"No, let's find a place to eat. I'll take over the driving. How far are we from Houston?"

"I figure we got maybe another few hours."

After Coke, coffee, and sandwiches, they were back on the road. It was sunset. The sun was behind them and the winds had died to a light breeze. It was no longer cold, just a slight chill in the humid air. They still had several hours on the road, but the humidity and the smells of vegetation was a sign that they were getting closer to the gulf.

Naomi was driving when they pulled up into the senior Gallagher's driveway. According to the radio, it was 80 degrees in Deer Park, Texas. Myra and Bryan were both sitting in their wooden rocking chairs. Popping the trunk, she grabbed the luggage while the boys ran up to their grandparents on the porch. In unison, the boys yelled, "Grandma, Grandpa, we are here."

Denny was the first to ask. "Grandpa, what does it feel to have a new lung."

Naomi turned to her oldest son. "Denny… that is not very nice."

"It is all right, Naomi." Turning back to the boys who were just standing there looking at their grandfather, he said, "Boys, that is the very first question I had when they told me that they wanted to give me an overhaul. I'll tell you right now, it feels kind of weird. I mean I've been hooked up to that oxygen tank for a few years now. Now I've got it in the house, but only if I feel I need it."

"What about the new heart, Pop?"

"Well, son, so far so good. I had to promise I would exercise every day."

"You mean like your neighbor and run every day?"

"No, Russell, I was told not to overdo it. For right now, I just need to take nice leisurely walks."

"Okay, children, let's go inside. I've got a little snack for you guys. I didn't know if you'd be hungry, so there is bread, cold cuts, and mustard or mayo. Pickles if you want." Myra gave a quizzical look at her son.

"Mom, that sounds great."

Myra glanced over at her husband, then to Naomi, "Tomorrow is Easter Sunday. Will you be going to mass with us?"

Russ spoke up. "Yes, Mom, that sounds great." Putting his arm on Naomi's shoulder, he said, "Doesn't it, Naomi?"

Looking directly into his blue eyes and with very little enthusiasm, Naomi said, "Yeah, Russ, that sounds great. Right now after I have a sandwich, I am going to crash."

Russell just shrugged his shoulders. "Mom, I'm sure she will want to go to church."

Myra first glanced at Bryan, then with a hand covering Russell's, she said, "It's all right, Russell. You guys have been through hell. I cannot even imagine what it must be like. The worse thing I ever had to worry about with you kids is when you all had the measles at the same time."

Glancing at the little breakfast nook, then a second look, Russell shook his head and rubbed his red eyes, "Wow! Gray skirt, pink blouse. I never thought you needed make-up, but with what you have on you look great. What, you didn't bring your heels? Although the black pumps—or are they loafers—look great. Me, I had to dig in my suitcase for my cleanest dirty pullover shirt and slacks that didn't look like there were slept in."

"Well, Russ, you do what you can with what you got. You want to see how the boys are coming along? By the way, Russ, if you look in that suit bag you will find a pair of khakis and a nice button-down tan shirt."

Before Russ was able to walk back to the bedroom where the boys spent the night, the boys actually skipped into the kitchen. "Mornin', parents."

Looking over at his wife, Russ said, "Where did you keep those clothes for the boys?"

"Kept them in the suit bag with mine. Same place I kept your stuff," replied Naomi.

Bryan's breathing seemed a little labored. "Dad, you doing okay?"

"Well, son, I've felt worse. Don't know what's going on. Maybe I just need a cup of coffee."

Myra came out in a nice power blue pant suit with her heels in her hand, studying her son, daughter-in-law, and the boys. "Myra, you look great. The boys are looking good, but Russell, not so good."

"Mom, I'm going to change."

Everyone looked at Bryan. Myra asked, "You doing all right, Dad?"

"Yeah, Myra. I'm okay now. Don't know what happen."

Surprisingly everyone was ready and they were able to make the 8:00 AM mass. The parking lot at the church was not that crowded. "I do think there may be a problem parking at the 10 AM and 12 PM masses. Many of these people only show up twice a year: Christmas and Easter with the occasional baptism," commented Myra.

"Sounds a lot like my dad. Seems like the older he's getting, the more he attends church. My mom says that that he hasn't missed a Sunday or holy day of obligation mass in the last two years," replied Naomi.

Myra and Bryan marched the family down the center aisle to the second pew from the front. The younger Gallaghers would have been quite satisfied somewhere near the rear of the church. Anthony kept looking back at the cry room.

The priest's white vestment trimmed in gold seemed to all but sparkle. Before stepping down from the ambo, the priest looked into the congregation, "*Haec dies quam fecit Dominus*: This is the day which the Lord has made. Throughout the octave we shall sing of the unequalled joy which throws open eternity to us. Every Sunday will furnish a reminder of it, and from Sunday to Sunday, from year to year, the Easters of this earth will lead us to that blessed day on which Christ has promised that He will come again with glory to take us with Him into the kingdom of His Father."

Back at the senior Gallagher's house, both Denny and Anthony were high-spirited. Bryan and Russ were in an animated conversation, and Myra was busy briskly moving about the kitchen. Naomi appeared sullen and withdrawn.

He noticed Naomi with a full cup of coffee, but did not make any attempt at drinking the coffee. "Naomi, what's the matter?"

"Oh, Russ, today is supposed to be what it's all about. I mean, we celebrate the Resurrection. Everything is supposed to be roses. I just can't celebrate when I don't know what is happening to my baby. I don't know where she is, if she is being hurt. Oh, Russ, I don't know if I can handle much more."

Myra ran cold water over her hands from the kitchen sink and wiped them with one of the dishtowels. Glancing back at Naomi, she said, "I know it's not very sanitary, but in fifty years of marriage, I don't think Bryan or Russell ever got sick from anything in my kitchen—that includes me."

Wiping her eyes with the back of her knuckles, Naomi said, "Oh, Myra, it is not you or your home. I miss my baby. We will be leaving early tomorrow, and I honestly have to tell you that I'm going to miss your home and this house. You and Bryan too. Bryan gave me a little scare this morning. But it looks like Bryan is doing much better. I see the two men have found something to disagree on—probably sports."

Myra gazed over at Naomi, then lifted her head. "You know, I was envious of you and Russ."

"Myra, why in the world would you be envious of us? You and Bryan seem to have it all together."

"Well, Naomi, one thing: you and Russ have a wonderful family. God never saw fit to bless me with more than one child. Don't get me wrong. Bryan has been a wonderful husband. Sometimes I wished he could have been more demonstrative. You know, it would have been nice to get the occasional hug, even in public. But you guys…"

"I'm just going to let the kids work off some of that energy. That includes the big kid. You know your son."

"Are you going to try and drive straight through?" asked Myra.

"You know, I know better than to push myself on the road, but with everything that has happened, I'm just a little shell shocked about stopping any place. Russ and I can take turns driving, but there are things a body needs to do, so I'm sure we will be stopping."

* * *

A couple of roadside rest area stops and several hamburger and the Gallaghers where pulling into the drive in St. Pete.

"Denny, think you can give me a hand with some of this luggage?"

"Give me a minute, Dad. I really gotta pee," replied Denny.

Anthony, standing next to Russell and looking up, said, "I can help."

As she dumped the dirty clothes out next to the washing machine, she saw Denny and Anthony spread out in front of the TV. Russell, with a glass of iced tea in his hand, was lying in his recliner when Naomi caught the full glass of tea just before Russ was about to let the glass fall out of his hand. Naomi went into the laundry room and put the dirty clothes in the washing machine and just closed the lid.

Standing in the middle of the living room and taking in the sight of her sleeping family, she announced, "All right, everybody! Who wants food?" No answer. "Then let us all retire to our beds." Both boys rubbed their eyes. Russell yawned and stood up. "Tomorrow is a big day. Dad, you need to sign in at the air base, and you boys need to get back to school. I have to check with my boss to see if I still have a job."

* * *

Sitting in front of a desk with a very skinny major, Russell was starting to feel like that dog that people used to put in the back window of their car, just to watch the head bounce up and down. It took him a few minutes to realize the major—Major Wiley, the squadron commander— was actually asking him a question. "Sir?"

"I was saying that I don't think you have filled out this emergency data form."

"Sir? Major Wiley, I'm not sure what you mean. I've put down my name and address and my wife's name. The names of my kids. I really don't know what else you want."

"I'm sorry, Sergeant, but I need your personal e-mail address."

"Sir, I don't own a computer."

"Master Sergeant Gallagher, you must be the last person on earth without a computer."

"My wife uses one for work. I'm competent with the use of the programs we use in the air force. We used a computer in Fallujah to flight follow. I've used the computer to run the numbers and aircraft times and monitor metal fatigue and pilot crew rest. We also monitored pilot medical records. To answer your question, once out of the air operations center, I just wanted to stay away from the electronic devil."

"Well, Master Sergeant, you need to become so familiar with the new cyber air force that you will be operating a computer in your sleep. Not only that. I need you to understand the workings of our new cyber air force. Do you understand, Master Sergeant? You know, now in the twenty-first century, we also keep our publications updated on our computers."

"Yes, sir. I assure you I will be current in the use of computers."

"And?"

"I will make sure to get up to date on the cybernetics."

"Thank you. Tech Sergeant Granger is expecting you. He's over at Command and Control. I need you to get up to date as soon as possible."

"Yes, sir."

"By the way, I heard rumors that you are dealing with personal problems?"

"Yes, sir, my lit—"

"Sergeant, I do not want to hear it. You got problems, you leave them at home. Now get out of here."

Russell stood and turned to walk out of the major's office. "Oh, Master Sergeant, I meant to ask…"

"Yes, sir?"

"What were your job assignments while in the desert?"

"Sir, I worked flight management. I made it possible for our flying personnel to stay current and up to date on air force publications having to do with flying."

"I do have one more question. How did you get assigned to Command and Control?"

"I am not sure, sir, but I will do any job assigned to me to the best of my ability."

"All right. Check in with Tech Sergeant Granger."

As he entered a building with a sign over a gray metal door, and the words in black over a white sign telling everyone that this is the command post, Russell noticed a large, heavy blond tech sergeant. He stood and walked toward Russ with his hand out. "In case you haven't guessed, I'm Tech Sergeant Granger." Looking down at his protruding belly, he added, "And after 16 years the air force has decided that I should find another occupation."

Russ looked directly in the other man's pale blue eyes. "I take it that it wasn't your idea to leave the air force."

"You're right, but like I've heard, you can't cry over spilt milk."

"I often wondered just what that meant."

"I have no idea."

"Master Sergeant Gallagher, would you like coffee, a soda, maybe a bottle of water?"

"No, I'm fine for now."

"I take it you got the big speech about this being a new improved cyber air force. Don't let it scare you. You have some good troops here, and they will help you in any way they can." Clearing his throat and letting out a breath, he added, "They will do anything to keep Wiley Coyote out of here."

"What about during flying ops or exercises?"

"Well, the pilots don't want him around. Our wing commander doesn't really want to be around him. So he's given busy work and told to stay in his office. He wears command pilot wings and is occasionally scheduled to fly the backseat."

"I'm surprised I didn't have to check in with the wing commander."

"Oh, he's at some kind of conference."

"Just in case anybody asks, what's the wing commander's name?"

"Sorry 'bout that. Paris. His name is Paris—Col. Dwight Paris."

"Okay... Let me give you the bus driver's tour." As they walked toward a metal door, Russ noticed a sign written in English and Spanish with the words that deadly force will be used on any unauthorized person entering this room.

"One other thing, Russ."

Scratching his head, he said, "Okay, Cyrus, what is that thing?"

"Our job description. You're an operations specialist. I'm a command and control supervisor. Our job is unique..."

"Okay. Please go on. We are not only to babysit pilots and typical air crews. We also take care of other command and control specialists. If you hadn't noticed, we fly AWACS, and we have command and control and radar specialist airborne."

Opening the door, Russ felt as if he were entering a movie theater. The lights were down. There was subdued lighting behind a white board that was above a little raised platform, which looked to Russ like a little stage. On entering the room, Russ noticed a red phone with no button or dial at the end of the console near the entrance. The other two positions had audio jacks where head phones could be plugged in. To the left and behind the console was a glassed-in room with audio jacks for head phones. On the far end of the console inside the glassed-in room with another console was a digital phone. In the middle of the console was a radio with both VHF and UHF—ultrahigh frequencies. Next to that radio was another radio.

Cyrus explained. "This is our secure radio. Every day a different code is entered into the radio, sometimes several times a day. It works with the aircraft radios by constantly changing frequencies. Supposed to keep the bad guys from intercepting our pilots' radio calls." Pointing to each end of the console, Cyrus remarked, "We also have flight strip holders."

There was an office on the far end of the command post. Sergeant Granger motioned for Russ to follow him. He was standing in front of a desk with a standard-sized desktop computer with a 21-inch monitor on a moveable shelf that went under the desk. The computer was also under the desk but set back, apparently so someone could sit at the desk without cracking their shins. There was another desk with a normal-sized desktop computer with a printer beside it. "Okay, Russ. You don't mind if I call you Russ, do you?"

"Only if you let me call you Cyrus."

"Sorry, my mother used to call me Cyrus." With a chuckle, he added, "Just call me Cyrus, or if the brass is around, call me Tech Sergeant Granger. Now let me explain the computers. The computers in the command post are secure and on the air force secure line. As we entered the office, the first computer was set up on the worldwide web. The one next to the printer is used like Quick Books. We can create spreadsheets. We also use that one for schedules and can be used like a Word program. The servers for the secure computers are in that room next to the office."

"Okay, I got it." Looking for at least a little smile, he said, "You know, I have no idea what you just told me. I may be calling you from the gate just to find my way out of here."

"You'll be fine. Airman Wills, our admen specialist, will be in tomorrow. Staff Sergeant Jones is the duty controller tomorrow. Either one of those guys can help you navigate our—what is it our leader calls it? Oh, yeah. Our cyber air force. I'm off for the next two days. But just in case, I'll give you my personal phone number."

Crossing the Gandy Bridge, Russ was trying to organize his thoughts, thinking about his first day at his new assignment. *Not much different than the many first days I had in the many schools I attended growing up. That is until my dad retired and I actually started high school and finished in the same school. And no matter what duty station, there was always someone that seemed to go out of their way to make things difficult. The one thought that always helped was the fact that people in the military still get transferred. Why was I assigned to the command post? I'd heard of people in the army being assigned out of their designated job codes. Unless the air force is getting desperate for bodies. I've been in air operations and flight management for over ten years. In all these years I never once wondered about those AWACS people.*

He had spaced out, as the kids would say, so as he reached the summit of the bridge, the sun hit his eyes. He reached for the sun blinds and pulled down his sunglasses when he noticed the sun reflecting off a car on the far side of the bridge. Squinting into the sun, he caught a glimpse of a light rack on the roof of the car. Looking down at his speedometer, he said, "Shit," seeing the needle of the speedometer was at 90 miles an hour. Gently tapping his breaks, he managed to bring the car down to 60 miles. Passing the police officer, he heard the quick short blast of a siren. As he looked back, it didn't seem as if the police officer was following him. *That is all I need. Finding out the job description of the job I'm expected to do is as clear as mud. Learning about computers other than how to turn them on, write reports, checking the weather and flight following. Cyrus Granger mentioned code, whatever that means.*

Pulling into the driveway, he saw Naomi coming to the door with a smile, the kids in a better-than-normal mood. "Good evening, Gallagher family. You guys seem to be in unusually good spirits."

"Well, husband, it was not all bad. The boys got a ride in a taxicab this morning; so did I, by the way."

Putting his hand under Naomi's chin, Russ said, "I'm so sorry. We need to see about getting a second car."

"It's okay, Russ. There is no real hurry. Nancy, an attorney I work with, will pick me up and take the boys to school and me to work. She's a partner in the firm so she pretty much runs her own hours. Won't last for long, but maybe long enough to acquire another car."

* * *

After six weeks and several headaches while reading the command post manuals, procedures, and specific rules and regulations, he was finally beginning to understand the operation of command and control. In short, the command post was to act as the eyes and ears of the commander.

Col. Paris had returned from his conference at the Southeast Sector located at Tyndall. Russell was spending more time with the wing commander than he was comfortable with. The colonel was more than patient with Russell.

He was starting to spend more time in his office at command and control. He was used to taking off for lunch and either eating at what used to be an NCO Club but was now called the Enlisted Club. Russ was pondering to himself, *I was excited when I became an NCO. I enjoyed the recognition and special privileges of being a non-commissioned officer. Now to be politically correct, everyone is treated the same.*

This morning Naomi had made him tuna salad sandwiches. He had gone to the coffee lounge to eat but thought that if he brought his coffee back to his office, he could work on bringing the pubs up to date and the controller schedules as one of the controllers was due to go on leave.

Walking into the office, he was aware that Airman Wills was just about glued to his computer monitor. Looking over his shoulder, he was surprised to see the airman watching hard-core porn. Noisily clearing is throat, he tapped Wills on the shoulder. "Airman! Just what are you doing?"

"Hey, Sarge, have you ever seen anything like this?"

"I'm not a prude, Airman, but I really don't think you are allowed to do that on duty."

"This is my lunch break."

"Aren't you comprising the computer system?"

"No, this computer is not hooked up to the Air Force Net or the base net."

"Airman, I don't want to see that in here again."

"Whatever."

Russ took his coffee and his sandwich and went back to the coffee lounge. He thought, *Now I know why I have never had a computer in my house.*

* * *

It was still very hard for Russ and Naomi to focus on a job. No wonder Naomi could feel the pain in the pit of her stomach. For Russ it wasn't much different. He liked an occasional beer and sometimes a scotch, but the beer was becoming daily. A weekend didn't go by that he did not finish a bottle of scotch.

It was a Saturday morning when the phone rang. Russ was already on his third scotch when Naomi picked up the phone. "Naomi, this is Asa."

"Asa?"

"Yes, Special Agent Asa Williams. Is Russ near?"

"Yes, yes. Have you found Jackie?"

"Sorry. I just wanted to check in with you and let you know that we have not forgotten about you or your little girl."

"I'm putting the phone on speaker." Turning to Russ whose eyelids were half closed and whose empty glass was just about to fall out of his hand, she said, "Russ, its Agent Williams."

His head popped up. "Have they found our baby?"

"No."

"Listen, Russ, has the agent there in Tampa been keeping in contact with you?"

"I don't even know his name, but the FBI did call about half a dozen times. Has anybody found anything about our child?"

"I am so sorry. I do want to assure you that Tom and I have not forgotten about you, and anything that has come through. We have had a few promising leads."

"Asa, it is becoming all I can do just to stay focused. My life is falling apart. I can't concentrate. And believe it or not, I'm much better off than my wife. I can tell the boys are having their own problems. Their grades have dropped. Anthony doesn't go outside much, but he does have his friends, which I no longer see. I think he tells them to just stay away. Denny is doing a little better. You know, I think the worse part for all of us is the not knowing."

"Russell, I can only imagine what you are going through, but I still think we have a better-than-good chance of getting your little girl. There has been a lot of activity on the Crow Reservation. It doesn't sound so good for them, but several more young girls have come up missing, Young women too."

"That doesn't sound good at all."

"I feel it means that Jackie's still alive. I don't believe she has been harmed?"

"Why. Why Asa. We have not been contacted about money. I'm only a master sergeant in the air force. I suppose someone might think I have access to government secrets. I don't. So why my little girl?"

"I have a few thoughts. Just don't you give up hope?"

"Thanks, Asa. I'm beginning to feel that our case has been put at the bottom of a very large stack."

"If it is any consolation, I have not stuck your case on the bottom of a large stack. Even when they try to take me off the case, or assign me additional work, Jackie is the first person I think of when I wake up and the last person I think of before I collapse at night. I gotta go now. I may be coming your way soon. Good-bye, Russell, I will be seeing you soon."

Walking out of the bedroom, Naomi stopped when she noticed Anthony sitting on the couch. "Anthony, what are you doing? You gave me a fright. I didn't know you were there." Looking in his lap, she noticed a rather thick hard-covered book. "What are you reading?"

Looking up at his mother, he said, "I'm sorry, I found this book on the bookshelf in your bedroom. Right now I'm reading about Padre Pio."

That's okay. You can read it, but I think you need to get closer to the light."

"I was 'fraid that you would be mad 'cause I went into your room. I heard you and dad talking on the phone. Was that the FBI man?"

"Yes, Anthony. He just wanted to let me know that he was still on the case. He thinks he knows where she might be."

"I know where she is." He looked up at his mom. He could see that her face was getting red. "But Mommy, I do know."

"Anthony, stop that. There is nothing about your sister being missing that is funny or cute. Even if this invisible friend of yours told you." With her hands on her hips, she added, "Anthony, I know you miss your sister, but I am really starting to get mad at you. I really don't need you making up stories."

"Sorry." Opening his book where his finger was, he thought, *She's my sister. I know where she is. I'm almost 8 years old. Nobody will listen to me.*

CHAPTER 14

S am Whitehorse could not have picked a better time for his mini-vacation. He and Rides the Horse had received suspensions. Nathan said that they should have been fired. The only thing that came to Sam's mind was, *It's a good thing there are not that many people that actually would like being part of the tribal police.*

It wasn't a bad time to be on vacation. Summer in Montana is great. He was sitting on the little metal steps leading up to his single-wide trailer. Comments had been made about his home. Like if any more rust spread on his home, he'd be enjoying the rising sun. He really didn't think that was all that bad a thing to happen. His grandfather would not die until his grandmother called the family together and moved him outside.

He had a can of warm beer. On the can was comment that it was locally brewed. Sam's taste were not that discerning, but if he had anything to do with brewing that beer, he sure wouldn't tell anyone. The door to the trailer was shut, but he thought he heard his house phone ringing. He had a cell phone; it was on his dresser. The ringing stopped. No, it started up again. "Ah," he sighed, dragging himself up the steps and into the oven that was his trailer. By the time he picked the receiver up, the ringing stopped. He opened up windows—at least the ones that he could open. A few of the windows were stuck closed. He had been meaning to work them lose or break them.

He was heading for the room he used as a bedroom—the one where he left his cell phone—when the phone started ringing again. Picking up the receiver, he said, "Yeah, this is Whitehorse."

"Whitehorse, is that the way you talk to your boss? Oh, hell, is that the way you were taught to talk to your elders?"

"Nathan, I still have a week left of my suspension."

"I know. I need you to come in. I've been trying to reach Rides the Horse. No answer. Nobody has seen him. If you could get hold of him, I'd like him to come in."

"Lieutenant, I haven't been near the station. So whatever happened, it wasn't me."

"Sam, you've done your time and you are not in trouble. Paula's teenage daughter is missing, so is Little Tree's daughter. They're both teenagers. Now Paula's kid has been a handful, but Little Tree's daughter has always been a good kid."

"How old are they?"

"They're both 16. If they had only been missing for a day or so, I would think they just ran off with their boyfriends. Ellen doesn't have a boyfriend."

"I think I know where Robert is. He likes to go into the mountains. He is very hard to find, but when we were boys I tracked him to his favorite trout fishing spring. He used to set up a lean-to, but not too long ago he talked about building a cabin," replied Sam.

"Sam, get in here as soon as you can. You're to partner up with Rides the Horse."

"Nathan, I would rather do it myself. I don't need a partner. I mean, we're looking for missing kids. Right?"

"Got a feeling, Sam. You know that little girl came through here and was taken right from under our protection. This is not the first time people have been missing from the Rez, but I got a feeling."

"Okay, Nathan. I'll stop by before I head for the hills. If Rides the Horse is where I think he is…"

"Yes, go on."

"It's a two-hour drive and then another hour walk."

* * *

On the road out of Woodland Park, Colorado, Darlene reached over and grabbed Melvin's arm. "Melvin, Melvin, look at me."

"Darlene, you want me to drive off this mountain? What do you want?"

"I don't like this van. I liked the van we had."

"If they haven't, I'm sure they will be looking for the old van. Besides, this van does not have any rust, and it drives real good. We got to go back to Montana."

"I thought we couldn't go back."

"I no sooner charged the cell phone and it started playing that damn music. It was vibrating all over the dresser. Larry has a job for us."

"Melvin. I don't like that Larry guy."

"Well, get over it. We need to go back to the Rez. There's a package for us. It has already been wrapped. I understand the package is real quiet."

"Is it going to be like picking up that little baby? The last time I saw that baby she was in the hospital."

"We're picking up two stoned teenage girls."

"Melvin, if the cops see us, we will be arrested."

"We won't be there that long, and besides they're not lookin' for a caravan.

Coming onto the highway, they headed for Colorado Springs. Melvin pulled the van off the highway and into a small residential area. Finding a little park, he parked the van and stepped out, walking over to a small ledge overlooking the highway.

Darlene opened the passenger-side door. Looking over at Melvin, she asked, "What are we doing here? Melvin, there are clouds below us."

Opening the door and stepping out, Melvin took several deep breaths. "Darlene, come on. Step out here and breathe some of this rarefied air. We should be able to see clouds below us. We are seven thousand feet above sea level."

Looking down on Pikes Peak Highway, then carefully walking around the van to stand next to Melvin, she said, "I thought you said we needed money, and your friend wanted you to pick up these kids right away."

"As usual, you are right, but we have enough money to get to Montana, and the girls, from what he told me, are resting."

"They are teenagers. They won't be resting long."

"I don't know exactly what they were given, but they will be in la la land for a while."

"Okay, Melvin. Where do we take them?"

"We will be told when we get there. There is cash waiting for us when we get back to Montana.

"Well, Darlene, I think we must be getting on our way. I wonder if it would be safe to go back to our place."

"Melvin, I always let you do what you think is best, and I sure could use some of my stuff. No, I don't think we should go anywhere near Lodge Grass."

"From what Larry told me we don't need to go anywhere near Lodge Grass or the agency. The girls are being held in Helena."

"Melvin, our old van had a closed-in cargo area, no windows. This minivan has windows. Windows from the front to the back. We had enough trouble trying to hide that three-year-old."

"First, Darlene, this is not a minivan, it's a caravan. From what Larry told me, these kids will be drugged. They spent a couple of days drinking beer and smoken dope. You know, Larry is a real doctor. Once the kids got real high, he gave them both a shot and a pill. He told me they would be awake but would do whatever they were told, plus they won't remember anything. All the windows on the caravan I had darkened, at least as much as the law in most states allow."

Raising her eyebrows, she said, "Never heard of anything like that… What if we get stopped?"

"We'll make it like a game. They will do what we say, whatever we tell them to."

* * *

From the tree line Sam was watching Robert, who was in water up to his waist, wearing rubber waders, a red flannel shirt, and trying to fly-fish like a white man. Moving stealthily from the tree line down to the edge of the water, he said, "Brother Ride the Horse, does that work better than the way our fathers taught us?"

Almost falling in the cold spring water, Rides the Horse answered, "Whitehorse, what are you doing up here?"

"Nathan needs us."

"I'm on suspension, and why does he need both of us?"

"I asked him the same question. I was sitting on my doorsteps with a cold brew, just pondering the Big Sky, when he disturbed me. Seems like someone is weeding out our tribe. Little Tree's daughter and his daughter's friend are missing."

"The other girls wouldn't be Paula's?"

"How did you guess?"

"They both probably ran off with their boyfriends. They'll show up."

"I don't think so. Not this time anyway. I mean, before I came up here, I checked out all the spots the kids like to hang out."

"One last cast."

The fly barely hit the surface of the surging waters when a large one jumped right on the hook. Throwing the trout in the small wicker basket hanging from a leather strap around his neck, Rides the Horse said, "You want to share him? Got a little fire right around the bend. Of course, we could always throw him back."

"Why not some of this fish? Don't take that long to cook. Maybe that white man has something with that fly fishen'."

Pushing his long black hair over his shoulders and tying it back with a piece of line, Sam said, "It looked like you were enjoying what you were doing."

"Beats the hell out of staring at four walls."

* * *

Sam and Robert were standing in front of the old splintered desk when Nathan Green— Lieutenant Nathan Green—looked up from a large pile of crime reports. Sam looked down and noticed they were all of missing girls, some women from the agency and Lodge Grass. Nathan reached to the side of the desk and handed two missing child reports to Sam. "I see you guys making faces at my old splintered desk, but this old maple splintered desk was here long before I went off to Vietnam, and from what I've been told, one of the first tribal police chiefs sat behind this desk."

Rides the Horse spoke up. "Sorry, Chief."

"How many times do I have to tell you not to call me Chief? Besides, unless you know something I don't know, I'm still a police lieutenant. Now I want the both of you to talk with Ellen's mother, Paula, and Sarah's mother, Mary Little Tree. I called down to the school and talked with the principal. He says they are both good kids, although Sarah is starting to notice boys. Ellen is a pretty thing but has not found any one boy that interesting, at least not yet. Her mom says she spends most of her time studying or playing soccer. I need you two to find out where the kids go and who knows them, besides the kids in school."

Paula was a single mother. Ellen had a brother. No one in the house had seen the father. The last Paula heard he was in jail. That was five years ago. She did know that he had been released but had no idea where he could be.

Sam was sitting on a worn couch in Paula's double-wide with his Stetson on his lap. Scratching his head, he looked over at Paula. "Do you think Ellen has had any contact with her father?"

"Listen, Sam, I know how kids are today, but Ellen has never even asked about her father. She hasn't mentioned him one way or another. I never badmouthed him, so I think if she had seen him she would tell me."

"Well, just to cover everything, what is his name?"

"His name is Joseph. He's a tall man with a scar under his lower lip. It almost makes a person think that he has two bottom lips. His name is Joseph Mitchell. His people live up near Yellowstone. I called up there, but they had no idea where he was. Sounded like they didn't want to know."

"Paula, do you mind if we look in Ellen's room?"

"Yeah, go ahead."

Sarah's mother, Mary Little Tree, was wiping her hands on a dish towel when Robert and Sam knocked on the door of a modest well-kept stucco three-bedroom house. "Sarah's dad died five years ago. He was working in the mines and was crushed when the mine collapsed. Sometimes he was away for a month, maybe longer. Then one day a white man in a nice gray suit came and told me he was dead. He left us some insurance, but I still had to go to work. Sarah is a good kid. She wants to go to college. She was hoping for a scholarship. I did smell beer on her breath, but that was last year. She told me she didn't like it and wouldn't do it again."

"Mary, would it be all right if we looked in Sarah's room?"

On the streets Robert and Sam found out that the two girls were friends. Seemed that whatever one did, the other had to do. They competed with everything: in school for grades and on the soccer field. Neither one had a reputation either with boys or drinking.

"Sam, I know we don't have jurisdiction off the Rez, but I know a place in Billings where kids like to hang out. Why don't we take a little ride into Billings?"

"What is that, about another twenty minutes? Why not."

"By the way, Sam…"

"What?"

"Your pocket is buzzing."

Holding the cell phone out away from his face and closer to Robert who was driving, he answered the phone. "Yeah, Nathan, I hear you. I wondered when you would suggest that. We got a hunch, and we're heading for Billings."

Robert glanced at Sam. "Well, what did he say?"

"Said he would call the local police, let them know we are coming. He also said he wants us out of uniform."

"Shit, this is all I got. I ain't got nothing but a threadbare pair of jeans and a sweatshirt."

Sam just shook his head. "What did you wear on your date the other night?"

"My uniform. I just took the badge off."

"Well, Rides the Horse, the lieutenant wants us out of anything that would say that we were part of the tribal police."

Rubbing his eyes, Sam said, "We need to go back to the agency so we can change. I think I might have something at the trailer that just might fit you. I have some clothes that I haven't been able to wear. It has been about four inches ago."

"That's great, Sam, but you are taller than me."

"They're jeans and you can roll them up."

CHAPTER 15

A few miles outside Billings, Melvin pulled the Dodge Caravan off the blacktop and onto a dusty narrow gravel road and then on a dirt road that looked more like a cow path. Smacking Darlene on the knee, he said, "See the log lean-to. Looks like where they might herd wild pigs. Well, Larry said they would be here."

Scooting up in her seat, Darlene observed, "Melvin, there ain't no people over there."

"Let's get a little closer."

Sure enough, looking into the darkened log shed, Melvin noticed movement. Climbing out of the Caravan and sticking his head in the darkened space inside the log shed, he called out, "Yow! Anybody in there?"

Just then he heard giggling. "I hear somebody back there. Larry sent us."

An old raggedy-looking white man with an untrimmed-looking gray specked brown beard, yellow fingernails, and yellowed blood-shot eyes came to the entrance to the log shed. Coming to the entrance and squinting into the sun, he looked up at Melvin. "Okay. So you're here. Are you ready to transport these two?"

"Larry said you'd have some money for us, and an address."

The old guy spoke, more like croaked, "Don't know notten about money. You're going to Chicago."

"Well, friend, I ain't goen' no place without money."

"Maybe I can give you a few dollars."

"Well, friend. You want for Larry to pay you? You give us enough money to get to where he is. The way I figure it, I don't get my travel pay, you don't get paid."

"I don't got no money. That little Arab said you had the money."

"Guess what? You get to keep the kids."

The bearded man pulled out a roll of bills, giving Melvin eight twenties and four fifties. "Okay. I don't need this. When you see your little Arab doctor, tell him not to try and get in touch with me again."

Darlene stood directly behind Melvin and kept slapping him on his back. "Melvin, where are these kids? I don't hear any kids."

Putting both his hands on the bearded man's shoulders, Melvin said, "You heard the lady. Where are the kids?"

Turning his head toward the darkness of the shed, the old man said, "Okay, sweeties, it is time for you to take a little trip."

One of the girls spoke like she had just woke up, "Is somebody gonna take us to West Wick Lane in Billings?"

The old bearded man got right into Melvin's face. "Okay, my lovelies, your chauffer is here."

Melvin stepped back several feet. This old man's breath smelled of decaying food or something dead. It was about to knock him out. "I thought there was two girls?"

"There is. Neither girl is feeling any pain. Chances are they'll sleep all the way to Chicago. If they do get restless, I've got a couple of these here, patches that the rag-head doctor gave me. Already put a patch on each girl. I'll give you a few more you can use ifen they get restless."

Darlene was staring at the baggies with the patches. "What are they?"

"Doc said the patches are Fentanyl. They're supposed to be like morphine, only the patches go into the bloodstream a lot slower than a shot or a pill."

* * *

"You know, Melvin, it's weird."

"What's that?"

"Oh, you know, we carried that little girl for a week, and even when she was sleeping I knew she was there. We got two teenaged girls, and they haven't made a sound. I mean teenaged girls are always giggling. They got that thing that makes them scream a lot."

"There is a rest stop just up ahead. I don't see any cars. I'll stop. Need to stretch my legs anyway. You go back there and make sure they ain't dead, or maybe in some kind of coma."

"Okay. How much longer to Chicago?"

"Well, it's over a thousand miles. If we drive straight through, it should take 'bout fifteen hours."

"Melvin, can you drive that long. Maybe we should stop for coffee or sumthin'?"

"As long as we got those kids, we won't be stopping. 'Sept maybe to pee. I guess we could switch out on the driven'. Just thinkin', maybe one of us could go into a store and get coffee."

Pulling the caravan onto the gravel on the shoulder of the road and riding the shoulder of the road to the entrance to the rest area, Melvin heard a moan from the back of the Caravan. "Darlene, did you hear that?"

"What?"

"I think one of the kids is awake."

Both girls were sitting up when Darlene slid the door open. "You girls need a drink of water. Maybe go pee?"

"Yeah, I could use some water. How come it is taking so long to get home?"

Handing a bottle of water to the girls, and then taking the bottle back, Darlene answered, "Oh, there was a bad wreck, and we had to wait for them to clear the road."

The smaller of the two girls—the one that hadn't said anything—replied, "Lady, I feel funny. Can't seem to keep my eyes open." Turning to her friend, she noticed that she was sleeping, and then the smaller one nodded and her head fell on her chest. Her breathing became deep and heavy and she was asleep.

Melvin pulled a map out of the glove box, taking it out of the Caravan and unfolding it. Attempting to spread the map, Melvin finally looked over at Darlene. "Looks like there is other rest stop up ahead. There should be a gas station about five miles up the road. I'll put the gas in and you go get us some coffee."

They were back on the road, this time with Darlene driving. Darlene put her head back on the head rest. She thought she heard something. There it is again. It sounded a lot like a puppy whimpering. Pulling onto the graveled shoulder of the road, with her head slightly turned, she yelled, "What's the problem back there?

"Lady, we both really got to pee."

"Okay, let me pull off the road." There were a few picnic tables just a few feet up the road. "I'm going to pull off near those picnic tables. You can pee there."

Rubbing his eyes with the back of his knuckles, Melvin said, "What are you doing, Darlene?"

"The girls got to pee."

Lowering his voice to almost a whisper, Melvin said, "You get out with them. We don't need them to try and run away."

The shorter of the two girls looked up at Darlene. "Lady, there is no restroom. Where are we supposed to go? Why is it taking so long to get to Billings?"

Pointing to a boulder near the picnic tables, she said, "Just go behind that rock."

"We're girls. We have to sit to pee."

Darlene lifted her arms and turned her palms up. "You can squat, can't you?"

Both girls went behind the boulder. They moved a few feet from one another, pulled their pants and panties down, and fell flat on their butts, saturating their panties and pants.

"Lady, lady." The bigger girl's speech was starting to slur. Both girls stood and staggered back toward Darlene and the Caravan.

"I can't keep calling you hey and hey you. What are your names?"

The larger girl responded. Pointing to her shorter friend, she said, "That is Sarah, and I am…" Just then her head dropped to her chest.

"Woo, I don't know what's happening, but I feel funny and I can't seem to stay awake. I drank beer before but it never did that me. Oh yeah, her name is Ellen. That boy gave me some weed. You think that is why I keep nodding off?"

All quiet in the backseat. By the time they reached Kenosha, Wisconsin, both Melvin and Darlene had stopped at least a dozen times. Neither one of the girls stirred.

"Darlene, you know this is where all the good beer comes from."

"As we crossed the state line, did you see all those cows? You know they make cheese here too." Turning around in her seat, she looked at the girls. They each had their head on each other's shoulders.

Melvin glanced over at a squirming Darlene and said, "What you squirming for? You got ants or some other bugs in your britches?"

"No… I just never seen anybody sleep like those two. I was getten' kinda worried. Sure wouldn't want to see them die on us."

Melvin was quiet, real quiet, for several minutes. "Ya know, Darlene, I don't think it would bother Larry one way."

Sitting up straight and rubbing her eyes with her fingers, Darlene asked, "What do you mean by that?"

"Just forget I said anything."

Darlene took a deep breath and turned to the window. Melvin couldn't see her face, but by the hesitation in her breathing, he knew she was sobbing. "Darlene, why the tears. You know what we do."

"Melvin, I always thought we was taken the kids to new homes. You know, rich people that want to empress their friends with kids. Make their friends think that the kids are theirs."

"You know what we do to make money. Some of the little kids are sold to people like pets. The older ones are sometimes used to work in rich people's homes. If they're pretty, they can use them on the street."

CHAPTER 16

Russell was sitting at the little kitchen table with a cup of coffee nestled in his hands. Looking at the clock over the kitchen sink, he said, "Oh, shit. We have a big exercise today. I need to get to the base." As he stood up, he cracked his knee against the table leg, and the cup dropped, splashing coffee down his leg and staining his khaki pants. "Just what I need."

Naomi looked up from the paper. "Calm down, Russ. I don't ever remember you being late. So if you're a few minutes late, it won't be the end of the world."

His face was getting red. He stopped and took a deep breath. "You know, you are right, but this guy I work for is looking for a reason to get rid of me."

After changing his clothes, Russ kissed his wife and waved at the boys on the way out. "I shouldn't be too late. You can never tell about these exercises, but they are just checking procedures, mostly my paperwork."

Naomi raised her head from the paper. "You want to take a cup of coffee with you?"

"No, Naomi. I do not want to take a cup of anything with me. I think I've had enough caffeine for the week."

Walking into the office, Russ saw that Airman Wills had his face buried into his computer screen, "Wills, has the old man been in yet?"

Startled, Airman Wills jerked his head up and attempted to shut down the computer. "No, boss. Just you, me, and the chickens."

Russ glanced over the airman's shoulder then stopped and stared at the monitor. "Wills, I thought we agreed for you not to do that here."

Spinning his desk chair around to face Russell, Wills said, "I did. I swear. I just booted it up and this is what came up. You got to see this."

Starting to walk away, Russ turned back and stopped. He froze at what he saw on the monitor. "What the hell is that?"

"It's some kinda auction, 'sept they're auctioning off people. Like what I read about in the history book. You know, I'm black and my folks told me about how my great-grandpa told those stories."

Moving Airman Wills out of his desk chair, Russ couldn't keep his eyes away from the screen. Then he saw it. It was a picture of his little girl. "Wills!"

"Yeah! I mean, yes, Sarge, what is it?"

"How can we find out where this is coming from?"

"I don't know. I guess there's a way to get an IP address, but I ain't that good yet. I think I can copy it and get somebody here that knows how to do it."

Russ pulled his wallet out and dug for a worn piece of paper. It had the number to the FBI. Fighting with the base operator to get an outside line, he said, "Operator, I can't get an outside line."

"No, sir, all the outside lines are down for this exercise."

Taking a deep breath and letting the air out slowly, Russ said, "Listen, this is Master Sergeant Russell Gallagher. I'm the NCOIC of the command and control here and this is part of the exercise."

"Sorry, sir. I'll put you through."

After several rings, someone answered, "This is the FBI. How may I direct your call?"

"Yes, this is Russell Gallagher. You people are investigating the disappearance of my little girl."

"What agent may I direct your call?"

"Special Agent Asa Williams was working the case."

After what seemed like an hour—more likely a few minutes—the operator came back on. "Sir, there is no Special Agent Asa Williams in this office. Do you have a case number?"

"I'm at work and all the paperwork to do with my daughter's abduction is at home."

"Sir, I thought you said your daughter was missing?"

"Yes, that is right. She is missing because she was abducted."

"Who is the lead agent on the case?"

"I told you, Asa Williams."

"We do not have a Special Agent Asa Williams in this office."

Getting frustrated, Russ said, "His office is in Baton Rouge, Louisiana."

"Sir, I can give you the number for that office."

"Ma'am, I was told that there would be an agent from the Tampa office assigned to my case. I did talk to someone, but I can't remember his name."

"Please hold, sir, while I connect with the senior agent."

Russell was still on the phone when Major Wiley, Colonel Paris, the ops officer, and several other officers arrived in his office.

Major Wiley tapped Russell on the shoulder, "Master Sergeant, the exercise is about to begin. We have two weather birds ready to launch. You will have to tell whoever that you will get back to them. You do know that I discourage personal calls while here."

"Sir, this is a critical phone call. You see my lit—"

"Master Sergeant, I told you on your very first day that I don't want to hear about your personal problems."

Just then he felt a vibration on his leg. His cell phone started ringing. "Major Wiley, I really do have to take this call."

Shaking his head, the major started to walk into the command post then stopped and turned toward Russell, "Master Sergeant Gallagher, you will report to me at the end of this exercise."

Stepping outside the command post, Russell heard the click on his cell as Agent Asa Williams answered the phone. "Mr. Gallagher, do you have information for us?"

"Yes, sir, I just saw a picture of my little girl on the computer."

"Did you get in touch with the agent in charge down there? I believe that would be Agent Zackery Taylor?"

"Sir, nobody seems to know who is in charge down here. To be honest and fair, Agent Taylor did give me a call."

"Give me your address. Tom and I will fly down there as soon as we get the jet cranked up."

Back in the command post, he observed people decrypting and encrypting messages. For the first time he observed the secure radio being used.

Walking back in the admin section, he tapped Airman Wills on the shoulder. When Wills turned his head back, Russ asked, "Wills, you know that stuff you showed me on the computer?"

"Yeah."

"Could you give me the website and show me how to get it?"

"Listen, Sarge, it was an accident that it came up. I really wasn't looking for it. I thought I might find a game."

"You're not in trouble. That little dark-haired girl that was on the computer screen is my daughter."

"Are you shitting me?"

"No. I am dead serious. You have to promise you won't tell anyone. I've called the FBI agent that is trying to get my little girl back. Can you help me?"

"I can do it, boss, but I will have to break some serious laws."

"I don't want you to get in trouble, but if you want I'll tell the powers to be that I was the one who made you do it."

"Naw. I think I can get it for you. It's what they call the Dark Web. Just let me know when the big-shots start coming around."

Russell's pocket started to vibrate and that god-awful music started to play. "Master Sergeant Gallagher."

"Listen, Mr. Gallagher, Tom and I will be landing at Pinellas Airport in about twenty minutes. You want to give me your home address again? We've got jurisdiction at the air base, but we don't really want to ruffle any feathers just yet. I'm going to set up our computers in the house. Do you have Wi-Fi?"

"I don't even know what that means, but Naomi works on a computer all day, plus she has a laptop. My boys can probably tear a computer apart and put it back together."

Just then Sergeant Jones stepped out the door and yelled, "Master Sergeant, the brass is looking for you."

Russell stepped into his office to see Major Wiley was waiting. "Master Sergeant, what did I tell you about personal calls? Now hand that phone over."

Colonel Paris walked into the office from the command post and eyed the major and then Russell. "Okay, Major. What is going on? If this affects our airborne AWACS, I need to know."

Major Wiley scrutinized Colonel Paris.

"Well, Major Wiley, what is going on?"

"Sir, the very day this airman signed into Wing I told him that anything personal was to stay at home, and I did not want to see his personal cell phone while he was on duty. He has deliberately defied me."

"Get over it, Major. Master Sergeant, what is the problem?"

"Sir… Colonel, my little girl has been abducted, and the FBI agent that is in charge of the case think he has a lead. He is on his way to my house right now."

The colonel, observing the major, then turned to Russell. "Master Sergeant, I want you on leave immediately. Call me if you need my help." Watching Russell scratching his head, he added, "Don't worry, Sergeant Gallagher, I can find someone to run your office temporarily. You've got a good team in there. I'm sure there is someone up to the task."

"Thank you, sir." As Russell was turning to leave, he noticed a grimace on Major Wiley's face.

In the parking lot, Russ felt a hand on his shoulder. Turning he saw the tech sergeant bent over with his hands on his knees, making sounds like he wanted to speak. Finally after taking a deep breath, he said, "Russ. What's going on?"

"I need to take a leave of absence. I just signed papers requesting emergency leave. The colonel already gave his approval."

"I was at the personnel office signing that little sheet of paper promising I would not tell anyone any air force secrets. All of a sudden the clerk picks up the phone, looks at me with a real strange look on his face, then says come back later. Colonel Paris wants to see you."

"I am so sorry, Cy, but there is a lot going on right now and I need some time to take care of it."

"I don't mind. Sally is going to be pissed. She has boxes all over the house. She has been packing and throwing things away for a week now."

"My daughter has been abducted. Airman Wills was looking at some website, and I happened to see a picture of my daughter. I have a special agent coming in today, but I sure could use some help finding that website?"

"Wills is good, but I am better. Already got a job lined up as an Internet technician with an insurance company. They don't expect me for a month."

"You know, we never did get together for dinner. Why don't you and Sally come over tonight and I'll introduce you to Special Agent Williams?"

Grabbing his little green memo book, Russ wrote his address down, tore out the page, and handed it to Cyrus. "Do you need me to draw you a strip map?"

"No, I can find It. I've been living off Vista in Tampa for the last three years. We're just a few blocks from Gandy, and you are not that far away. See you about 7 PM?"

"Sounds good. Again, I am so sorry about screwing up your life. You know for the first time in over a month I feel like something good is going to happen."

* * *

Russ was pulling up into the driveway. Before he could get out of the car, Naomi was at the car door. "Okay. Master Sergeant Gallagher, what is going on? Why are you home so early?"

"Me? What about you. Aren't you supposed to be working today?"

"Yeah. The school called me at work. The principal herself called. Seems like Anthony was acting out. So I had Nancy give me a ride. There was only an hour left of school so I brought them both home. Okay. I told you my story so you tell me yours."

"Several things happened to me today. First, I saw Jacquelyn."

With hazel eyes bigger than he had ever seen, Naomi glared directly into Russell's eyes. "Don't you bullshit me. I am in no mood, especially when you're talking about my baby."

"No, this is no bullshit. I was looking over the computer screen of one of my clerks, and there she was. I've already notified the FBI. Cyrus, my sponsor, is coming over tonight—he and his wife."

"Russell, you drop this on me then you expect me to entertain?"

"No, he is really good at computers. He is going to help us track down where Jackie is."

"Okay, wise guy. My laptop is in the bedroom, I wouldn't know where to start."

"That's okay, Agent Williams is coming over. There is a cyber-forensic team assigned to Tampa."

"Russell, I am really starting to get annoyed. Hell, not annoyed—I'm pissed. Will you please tell me what is going on?"

Come on, Naomi. The neighbors are starting to stare. Let's go inside. I need a glass of iced tea."

Before entering the kitchen, Naomi said, "Russell, no tea until you tell me what is going on."

"I called Agent Williams and told him what I saw. My clerk says he will try and help but he really only fell into the website by accident. The colonel told me to go home so I could concentrate on getting my daughter back. First it was going to be Asa and his partner. I called him back and told him what I found out about the website. So he is passing on what I told him to the cyber-forensic team."

Filling a glass with ice and pouring strong sweetened tea over the ice, Naomi handed the glass to Russ. "Well, this will certainly give our neighbors something to talk about. Not that I care."

"Naomi, I do not care either. I want our child back, even if I have to put search lights in our front yard. Asa said the operation will be discreet."

Literally dropping into the recliner, Naomi glared up at Russell. "So the colonel gave you time off. What, 24 hours?"

"No. He told me that I needed to take care of my family and I could take as long as I needed."

Cyrus and Sally Granger arrived about 6 PM. Naomi had sliced cold cuts and cheeses and prepared chips and condiments at the kitchen table. There were two large pitchers of cold tea, one sweetened and the other unsweetened, with a large ice bucket beside.

Cyrus was a rather large portly blond-haired man, while his wife Sally was a petite, shapely auburn-haired woman. She hung on Cy as they sat with their sandwiches on the living room couch.

At about eight a minivan pulled up in the Gallaghers' driveway next to Granger's Jeep Wrangler. Naomi came out to the minivan. "Asa, you know we could be friends under better circumstances."

Tom was climbing out of the driver's side. As Tom stood, Naomi hugged him. "Tom. You guys go on in the house. There are sandwich makings and cold tea on the table, ice in the bucket. Tell your friend in the backseat to come on out here."

"Sorry. That's Zackery Taylor. He's my other half. My twin down here in the Sunshine State. No, is not the 12th president of the United States."

Sticking her head in the door and looking at Zackery in the backseat, Naomi said, "Zackery, you don't have to hide in the backseat."

"I'll be right in, ma'am. Just need to make a couple calls."

"Naomi, I see you met my other half. Actually he is Asa's other half," commented Tom.

Naomi stopped and turned back to the minivan, "You aren't re—?"

"No, ma'am, as far as I know I am not related to President Zackery Taylor. But I have been told he did own slaves, plus I think he was a white dude," he said, smiling up at Naomi.

Zak came in with what looked like a leather carrying case. In the case was a laptop computer. Turning to Naomi, he asked, "I don't supposed you have Wi-Fi set up in here?"

"As a matter of fact, I do have Wi-Fi in this house. I'm supposed to work an eight-hour day, but there have been times I needed to take my work home."

Back and forth on the phone. Zak's fingers flying across the keyboard of his computer. Granger suggesting ways to find the Dark Web.

Zak's wireless phone rang. After a few nods and several grunts, Zak looked up. "Asa, Tom, our cyber-forensic tem has been tracking that IP address all over the world. We still have not been able to pin it down. Our cyber-forensic team seem to think it is located somewhere in Illinois."

Out of the corner, Naomi noticed Anthony get up and head for his bedroom. She motioned for Denny to follow him. "Denny, make sure your brother is all right. This is a little much for me. As a matter of fact, why don't you guys just get your nightclothes on and go to bed."

"But, Mom, it's early."

"Not really, but just get in bed. I'd tell you to turn the TV on but it may distract the people out here. Maybe you two can find a board game. Just promise to be quiet."

Denny responded with a very unenthusiastic "okay."

CHAPTER 17

Sam Whitehorse had his head back and his feet up in his worn leather recliner. His eyes were closed and it would appear the can of beer in his left head was about to slide out of his hand and spill the remaining warm beer on the scuffed linoleum floor of his single-wide trailer when his eyes opened with a start as he felt the warmth of a body. Turning his head to the left, he saw a young boy. His heart seemed to race. He hadn't realized that he was holding his breath until he inhaled the cool summer air from the open door of his trailer. What he saw was a very pale white-haired boy of maybe eight. The boy had his hand on his shoulder. When he felt he could finally speak, he looked into the boy's pale blue eyes, "Are you the one they call the Ghost who walks?"

He grabbed the can of beer before it fell on the floor.

"I don't know, but you know my sister. Nobody will listen to me. I know where she is. Someone has to get her soon. Something bad is going to happen."

Taking the warm beer out of Anthony's hand and putting his feet on the floor and sitting up, Sam asked, "What **do** they call you?"

"I am Anthony, and I am not a ghost. Can you help me help my sister?"

Sam stood up and tilted his head so he would not hit his ceiling. "Where is your sister?"

"She is in a big building. It might have been a factory or maybe a place where thy kept big things and boxes. Now there is a sign that says clinic. I think it says reproductive services underneath clinic over two big doors in front, and in the back is a fence, and beyond the fence is a very big lake. I thought it was the ocean, but I saw another sign that said Lakeside. I'm in the third grade and I can read pretty good."

"Anthony, I need more than that to find this place."

"There was another sign. It was a long word that started with a Wak—I couldn't read the rest but the second word was Illinois."

"I can find that, but if I'm right that is a long way from here."

"Mister Whitehorse, we need to hurry. There are all kinds of bad things in that building. Two sleeping teenage girls just came in. One might be dead."

"Anthony, I will get Rides the Horse and we will be there soon. I need you, if you can to keep whoever this is from hurting anybody else. Just don't want you get hurt. Maybe make noise or something. Do you know how to call the police?"

"Yes, of course I do. I'm eight. There are phones upstairs in the offices. I think they still work. I just got to push 911."

"Even if we can get an airplane out of Billings tonight, it will still take us several hours. I got a thought. Do you know what a fire alarm box looks like?"

"Yeah… yes, sir. One of the kids at my school pulled the alarm. Boy, did he get in trouble."

"Well, you are **not** going to get in trouble. Just don' get caught."

* * *

Zak was going through the different websites when Cyrus tapped his on the arm, "I don't really want to interfere, but cold I give it a try."

Zak motioned for Cyrus to sit next to him on the couch then handed the laptop to him. "Knock yourself out. So far I've been to Syria, Afghanistan, and a few places I never heard of. Our team over in Tampa is doing maybe a little better. I'm sure they will find the address, but it looks like it will take time."

Asa eyed Naomi. "Mrs. Gallagher, our boys look exhausted. Do you think you could put on a pot of coffee?"

Within minutes the smell of coffee permeated the house. Asa grabbed the cups that Naomi set out. Calling from the kitchen into the living room, he said, "How do you boys take your coffee." In unison, without taking their eyes off the computer screen, they answered, "Black and strong." Then they glanced at each other and laughed.

Naomi and Sally cleared the table and invited Special Agent Taylor and Cyrus to bring the laptop to the table where they would be more comfortable and closer to an electrical outlet.

* * *

Melvin pulled up close to a set of double doors. Under a large white sign in large block print were the words "Clinic," and under that were the words "Reproductive Services." Under that was in much smaller letters: "Waukegan, Illinois."

Darlene looked back at the girls. Sarah was barely sitting up. Ellen was slumped in the backseat. Darlene opened her door and slid the door to the backseat open. Motioning for Sarah to come out, she said, "Sarah, can you help me with your friend?"

"Is she dead? She is awfully cold."

Melvin stepped out of the Caravan just as a large black man pushed the two large doors of the clinic open. With a very loud and deep voice, he said, "Hey! You can't leave that there."

Melvin looked up, covering his eyes against the glare of the sun on one of the large picture windows to the right of the doors. "This is a women's clinic, right?"

The big black man was coming closer to the Caravan. "Yeah. You got an appointment?"

"They know we are coming. The doctor told me to bring these people here," countered Melvin.

"Well, you can't leave that van there," responded the black man. As big as the black man was, he had to look up at Melvin as he approached the van.

"No problem, but you get down here and give us a hand with these girls." Melvin slammed the door to the van and started walking closer to the black man.

As his eyes seemed to open even wider, he said, "Okay, mister. I'll help."

Darlene glanced over at the large man. "Could you get a gurney? I can't carry both these girls."

The black man just stood there, looking first at Melvin and then at Darlene. "Yes, ma'am."

Melvin looked as if he was about to burst a blood vessel in his neck. "Get the gurney and then come back here and help." Picking Sarah up and cradling her in the crook of his arms, he left Darlene with Ellen and called to the large black man. "Hurry, we need to get this girl inside."

Once inside the building and near two doors with a sign indicating that only authorized personnel were allowed beyond this point, there was a short dark man with a surgeon's cap, paper face mask, and a green surgical gown. Pulling his surgical gloves off, he asked, "What is all the commotion out here?"

The big black man spoke up. "Doctor! Dr. Labeed, these people said you told them to come here."

"Yes. Yes. Put the one on the gurney in the pre-op room and the other one in the room nearest the nurse's station. Have someone clear her up and put her in bed."

Darlene called after the doctor. "Are you the doctor? Please help her. I think she is dying."

Pulling down his paper face mask from his nose and mouth, he ordered, "Woman, bring that gurney over here."

Darlene, who was heading for the door that had a sign "Pre-Op" stopped and turned to face Dr. Labeed. With a whimper, and a sniffle, she said, "Are you talking to me?"

"Yes, woman. Bring her here."

Turning to look for Melvin and noticing him at a reception desk, Darlene yelled, "Melvin. Melvin, I need you."

With a deep breath, Labeed scrutinized Darlene then told her, "Follow me. Take a gown and paper face mask. Put the latex surgical gloves on. You're not allergic to latex, are you?" Glaring at her and then looking over at Melvin, he said, "Tell this woman to follow me."

Dr. Labeed was motioning to Darlene to stand down by the foot of the operating table and to make the young woman bring her knees up and for her to hold her feet. *

* * *

Anthony was in the building near two large garage doors. Anthony was thinking, *Those doors are big enough to back a locomotive in.* He was lost. This did not look that same as it did the first time he was here. *This has to be the place. Jackie should be in a big room. But I don't see any rooms. Before I pull a fire alarm, I have to be sure I'm in the right place.*

He found a stairway. There was an elevator beside the stairs. He took the stairs. When he got to the second floor, he saw doors that looked like office doors. He checked to see if they were unlocked. Most of the doors were locked. He did find one that was unlocked. There was a phone on an old dusty desk. There was a phone on the desk. It didn't have push buttons. It had a dial. He picked up the phone and there was no sound.

He came up to another stairwell. There were stairs that went up and stairs that went down. He stepped to where the stairs went up or down. He heard voices coming from below. He was afraid someone would see him, but he slowly creeped down the stairs. At the very bottom he saw a light. Holding himself against the wall, he peeked inside. He saw two people both dressed like doctors with green gowns and their faces covered with paper masks.

He heard two voices. The one sounded like the doctor he saw in Montana. The other voice was familiar, but he couldn't be sure. There was a phone on a desk not far from the two people dressed like doctors. Mr. Whitehorse told him to forget about the phone but to look for a fire alarm.

First, I have to find my sister. That big room I saw has to be closed. He waited for the two people dressed like doctors to leave the room. It seemed like it was taking forever. They finally walked out. There was a door on the far side of the room. It was not near the door the two people with doctor clothes went through. There was no window in the door so he had to open it a little bit. He didn't see any people but he did see another door, and it sounded like there were machines running in that room. He eased the door of the room that sounded like it had machines in it.

In the middle of the room was a big, very big oven. The oven was big enough for people to walk inside. It looked to Anthony like a big gas stove. He could see blue flames coming out of pipes with holes, like the gas burners on the stove in the house they used to live in.

There was no one in the room. There was another room. He walked to a room with a single metal door. He tried to open the door. To his surprise, it was unlocked.

In all this sneaking around he could not understand why it was so hard to find his sister. The first time he found her was in a little hospital in Montana. *Why can't I find her?*

At the third door he opened, he saw his sister had a tube down her throat and needles and tubes in both her arms and in her feet. There were tubes going into her nose and a machine that looked like it was oxygen air.

After looking to see if anybody else was around, he carefully went over to his sister. He put his hand on her arm. Her arm felt cold. He then put his hand on her head and bent down to listen to her breathe. She was breathing.

Now he had to find a fire alarm. He heard people coming. It was that short man and the woman. He could see their faces. That was the dark man he saw in the hospital in Montana. He remembered the woman. That is the woman with the mousy brown hair that his mom was fighting.

Anthony was still in the room with his sister. He was exploring the room and keeping his eyes on his sister. At first he was looking for the fire alarm. Then the more he thought about the situation, the more he was sure he had to get his sister out of this room. There were other kids in the room, some just babies, many younger than Jackie. Opening cabinets and drawers, he found scissors, a sharp thing that looked like something that the doctor might use to cut on a person, maybe to operate. He took the scissors and a small box of gauze. He took tape. Some were the sticky kind, then there was tape that didn't have any stickiness.

He thought he heard someone near the door. He stopped and hid under one of the beds. Whoever came in turned around and went out. All the people in the room were big kids and little kids. There were babies in incubators. They looked to Anthony like they were in plastic boxes with breathing tubes. The tubes were stuck in the babies like they were in Jackie.

Jackie was in the middle of the room. He was about to take the needles and tubes out of Jackie. *What if Jackie can't breathe without that tube in her nose? What if she needs the medicine that is coming out of the needles? Oh well, I got to get her out of here.*

As he took the needles out, Jackie started to moan. When he pulled the tube out of her throat, she coughed then gagged. It looked like she was about to throw up. She started to scream. Anthony put his hand over her mouth.

She squirmed and looked up at Anthony. "Antnie, where Mommy?"

"Be quiet, Jackie. You'll see Mommy real soon. Right now you have to stay quiet. Can you walk?" He tried lifting her out of the bed. She was stuck. Looking down, he could see that there were straps around her wrist. He couldn't figure out how to untie or unbuckle. He reached in the pocket of his jeans and pulled out the thing with the little sharp blade and cut the straps. He was surprised in how easily the blade cut the straps.

Jackie was having a hard time walking. Anthony half carried her, half dragged her to the door. Pushing the door open, he saw what he had been looking for: the fire alarm box. He thought all he had to do was pull a lever on the alarm box. With this alarm, he had to break a glass that was covering the lever. He hit the red box as hard as he could. It did not break. Little Jackie was squirming in his arms. She wiggled out if his grasp, picked up a metal doorstop, and swung her hand with the metal stop in it and hit the glass window. It broke. Anthony pulled the alarm. The screech of the alarm was bloodcurdling. The sprinkler system went off. Everything was getting wet.

Running to the closest stairwell, Anthony saw a door that was partially open. Squeezing in the door, he stepped into a bucket. There was a large metal sink in the room. They were in the janitor's closet. Lifting Jackie up in his arms, and trying to yell over the sound of the alarm, he said, "Jackie, you got to stay still and quiet."

Holding her, Anthony could feel her belly tighten and start to convulse. He held her over the big sink. She was throwing up yellow bile. She seemed to calm down He stuck his head out and didn't see anyone. He heard the fire engines outside. Looking out the door, he could see the hallway seemed empty. No people, no noise. "Come on, Jackie. Do you think you can make it?"

"Antnie, Jackie don't feel good. Jackie wants to go to bed. Jackie want Mommy."

"I know, but we got to get out of here first."

Keeping close to the wall, Anthony and Jackie were slowly making their way down the hall, when out of nowhere there was a very large black man coming right at them. The alarm stopped, but the black man's voice was deep and loud. "You kids stop. What are you doing here? Stop!"

* * *

Sitting in an aisle seat on a twin-engine propeller-driven airplane, Robert Rides the Horse could feel his knuckles turning to white from the pressure of his hands around the armrests.

"You know, Robert, there are more accidents in cars than on airplanes. I take that back. In your case, there are more accidents on horses than on airplanes," remarked Sam.

"Okay, wise guy. When are we going to get up in the air? I've been watching the dust that our propellers are kicking up since we left Billings," observed Robert.

"Robert, it really isn't that bad." He sat up straight and tightened his seat belt.

"Says you, as you tighten your seat belt. Sam, are you sure there is an airport near Waukegan?"

"I hope so. That is where this guy said he was going to take us. If he doesn't, Nathan is going to be pissed. I think he robbed the petty cash just to get us this far."

"Sam, you told me that we would have to pay our own way. I dug my share of the fare out of my sock drawer. We are going to get paid back for this, aren't we?"

"According to my little CI, we should be able to get our teenagers as well as the little girl that was abducted over at Health Services. When we do that, they will have to justify our getting at least travel money."

Glancing over at Sam, Robert said, "Oh well. You got to go in the army. You know I ain't never been no place but the Rez."

Glaring at Robert, Sam queried, "Didn't you spend some time in Lawrence Kansas?"

"Yeah, that was to go to a trade school, but I felt like I was still on the Rez, 'cept there was people from the desert, the planes. You know Navajo, Comanche, and Hopi. Lots of people from the Dakotas. Just one big reservation."

"You been to Billings?"

"Is that off the Rez?"

"Shut up. We are either about to land or the engine is on fire, and we are about to crash," remarked Sam.

"Ya know, Sam. Maybe staying of the Rez ain't all that bad," responded Robert.

CHAPTER 18

A nthony was in the building near two large garage doors. He was thinking, *Those doors are big enough to back a locomotive in.* He was lost. This did not look the same as it did the first time he was here. *This has to be the place. Jackie should be in a big room. But I don't see any rooms. Before I pull a fire alarm, I have to be sure I'm in the right place.*

He found a stairway. There was an elevator beside the stairs. He took the stairs. When he got to the second floor he saw doors that looked like office doors. He checked to see if they were unlocked. Most of the doors were locked; he did find one that was unlocked. There was a phone on an old dusty desk. It didn't have push button; it had a dial. He picked up the phone and there was no sound.

He came up to another stairwell. These stairs went down. He heard voices coming from below. He was afraid someone would see him so he slowly crept down the stairs. At the very bottom he saw a light. Holding himself against the wall he peeked in. He saw two people both dressed like doctors with green gowns and their faces covered with paper masks.

He heard two voices. The one sounded like the doctor he saw in Montana. The other voice was familiar, but he couldn't be sure. There was a phone on a desk not far from the two people dressed like doctors. Mr. Whitehorse told him to forget about the phone, to look for a fire alarm.

First I have to find my sister. That big room I saw has to be close. He waited for the two people dressed in scrubs to leave the room. It seemed like it was taking forever. They finally walked out. There was a door on the far side of the room. It was not near the door the two people in scrubs went through.

There was no window in the door so he had to open it a little bit. He didn't see any people but he did see another door, and it sounded like there were machines running in that room. He eased the door open and the sound of machines got louder.

In the middle of the room was a big, very big oven. The loud hissing noise he heard was the sound of the gas jets inside the large oven. A full-grown person could fit in that oven. He could see blue flames coming out of the gas pipes, like the gas burners on the stove in the house they used to live in.

There was no one in the room. There was another room. He walked to a room with a single metal door. He tried to open the door. It was unlocked.

In all this sneaking around he could not understand why it was so hard to find his sister. The first time he found her was in a little hospital in Montana. *Why can't I find her?*

The third door he opened, he saw his sister. There were the same dozen beds; six on either side. It looked as if the bed had sheets that were almost clean. His sister was in the middle of the room on the side farthest away from him. She had a clear plastic mask on her face, her hands were tied to the bedrails, needles and tubes in both her arms and in her feet. It looked like there was a tube in her nose.

After looking to see if anybody else was around, he carefully went over to his sister. Putting is hand on her arm; her arm felt cold. He then put his hand on her head and bent down to listen to her breathe; she was breathing. She was awake, but not moving. There was a sink beside her bed. It looked like a wash rag. He wet the washcloth and put it on her head. She stirred. He put his hand over her mouth. She started to squirm and fight, until she saw him. He put his finger to his lips; *Jackie be quiet.*

Now he had to find a fire alarm. He heard people coming. It was that short man and the woman. He could see their faces. *That was the dark man he saw in the hospital in Montana. He remembered the woman. That is the woman with the mousy brown hair that his mom was fighting.*

Anthony hid under his sister's bed. He didn't think those people would ever leave. They finally left. At first he was looking for the fire alarm. Then the more he thought about it, the more he was sure he had to get his sister out of this room. There were other kids in the room, some just babies, many younger than Jackie. Opening cabinets and drawers, he found scissors, scalpels; he knew they were scalpels, and they were sharp. He'd seen them on a doctor show he watched with his mom. He took the scissors and a small box of gauze. He took tapes, some were the sticky kind then there was tape that didn't have any stickiness.

He thought he heard someone near the door. He stopped and hid under a different bed. Whoever came in turned around and went out. All the people in the room were big kids and little kids. There were babies in incubators; they looked to Anthony like they were in plastic boxes with breathing tubes. The tubes were stuck in the babies like they were in Jackie.

Jackie was in the middle of the room on the side, away from the door. He was about to take the needles out, and the tube out of her nose. *What if Jackie can't breathe without that tube in her nose? What if she needs the medicine that is coming out of the needles? Oh, well, I got to get her out of here.*

Jackie started moaning when he pulled the needles out of her arms. When he pulled the tube out of her throat she coughed then gagged, and it looked as if she were about to cry. He thought for sure she was about to throw up. She started to scream. Anthony put his hand over her mouth.

She squirmed and looked up at Anthony, "Antnee, where Mommy?"

"Be quiet, Jackie. You'll see Mommy real soon. Right now you have to stay quiet. Can you walk?" He tried lifting her out of the bed. She was stuck. Looking down he could see that there were straps around her wrist. He couldn't figure out how to untie or unbuckle them. He reached in the pocket of his jeans and pulled out the thing with the little sharp blade, and cut the straps. He was surprised in how easily the blade cut the straps.

Jackie was having a hard time walking. Anthony half carried her and half dragged her to the door. Pushing the door open, he saw what he had been looking for, the fire alarm box. He thought all he had to do was pull a lever on the alarm box. With this alarm he had to break a glass that was covering the lever. He hit the red box as hard as he could; it did not break. Little Jackie was squirming in his arms. She wiggled out if his grasp, she picked up a metal doorstop and swung her hand with the metal stop in it and hit the glass window. It broke, Anthony pulled the alarm. The screech of the alarm was bloodcurdling. The sprinkler system went off, everything was getting wet.

Running to the closest stairwell, Anthony saw a door that was partially open. Squeezing in the door he stepped into a bucket. There was a large metal sink in the room; they were in the janitor's closet. Lifting Jackie up in his arms, and trying to yell over the sound of the alarm, "Jackie, you got to stay still and quiet."

Holding her, Anthony could feel her belly tighten and start to convulse. He held her over the big sink. She was throwing up yellow bile. She seemed to calm down He stuck his head out and didn't see anyone. He heard the fire engines outside. Looking out the door, the hallway seemed empty. No people, no noise. "Come on, Jackie. Do you think you can make it?"

"Antnee, Jackie don't feel good. Jackie wants to go to bed. Jackie want Mommy."

"I know but we got to get out of here first."

Keeping close to the wall, Anthony and Jackie were slowly making their way down the hall, when out of nowhere there was a very large black man coming right at them. The alarm was stopped, but the black man's voice was deep and loud. "You kids, stop! What are you doing here? Stop!"

Anthony had no idea where he was going. He grabbed Jackie, half carrying half dragging her, he ran with his sister. He ran away from the big man. The man that was chasing them reminded Anthony of one of the big football players he had seen. Anthony never knew how really big the football players were until his dad took him and Denny to a stadium to watch a football game.

It looked like a narrow hallway going off to the right. If he could make it to the hallway maybe he could find a place to hide. Pulling at a door at the end of the hallway, he saw what looked like a kitchen. It was the back door to an old cafeteria. There were dusty trays and an old steam table. There was a big gas stove, a grill, and next to the grill was an oven with two oven doors one on top of the other. The stove and grill were still warm. Somebody cooked food here.

On the side farthest away from Anthony and Jackie was what looked to Anthony like a walk-in cooler. Anthony carried Jackie to the cooler. He thought he heard the man coming. He wasn't sure whether the heavy breathing he heard was him or the big black man. They made it to the walk-in cooler. Anthony felt a rush of cool air as he pulled the door open. There were metal shelves inside the cooler on both sides. On the shelves were Styrofoam coolers. He pulled the top of one of the coolers open. In the cooler were several blue plastic bags of dry ice. At the end near another refrigerator door on the second shelf were three stainless steel wide mouth thermoses. "Antnee, Jackie thirsty." She reached for one of the stainless steel thermoses on the second shelf. "Me want a drink."

Anthony picked up the thermos; it was so cold that it felt like his hand was burning. With some effort he managed to unscrew the lid of the thermos. He put the opened thermos up to his nose, and took a whiff. Whatever it was gagged him. "No, Jackie. We have to wait. Right now we have to hide."

There was another refrigerator door at the back of the walk-in. When Anthony pulled it open all the shelves were covered with snow. "Jackie, let's try to be quiet. We can stand here by the door. Maybe we can find room on one of the bottom shelves."

* * *

After coming to a bumpy stop, watching smoke and flames come from each of the two propellers, and the smell of burnt rubber as the pilot must have been checking out his breaks. The sound of the engines changed from a steady drone to a high-pitched whine as the propellers were feathered just as they pulled into what must have been their assigned parking place.

Sam cracked his head as he went through the door to what was supposed to be the terminal. Putting his Stetson on and then taking it off abruptly, "Ow," he said.

Cocking his head then looking up at his friend, "Okay, Kemosabe, what now?" probed Robert.

"What?" with raised eyebrow, he questioned Sam.

Robert said, glancing at Sam, "At your age, and you never saw the 'Lone Ranger'?"

"Unlike you, Robert, the first time I saw a TV was when I went to the army."

"You do know there is more than one movie theater in Billings. The *Lone Ranger* is a movie now," commented Robert.

"Nathan gave me a letter to take to the local police," Sam stated as he pulled an envelope out of his shirt pocket and taped it.

"Okay. I give up. You're taking a letter to the local police."

"It's to inform the locals who we are and why we are here. Now what we have to do is find transportation," replied Sam.

Looking around the terminal, Robert spotted a counter with what appeared to be a man sitting at a desk behind the counter. His back was to them but it appeared his head was down on the desk. There was a sign over his head that indicated that they could rent a car.

Robert walked ahead of Sam to the counter where he saw a little bell. He tapped it and watched the man's head pop up, like a turtle sticking his head out of its shell.

The man sitting behind a desk stood up and approached the counter. "May I help you?"

With both his hands on the counter, Robert replied, "Yes. We need transportation and directions."

"I'm sure I can provide transportation, and if I can't tell you how to get where you need to be, I do have maps."

Moving up beside Robert, Sam pulled out his tribal issued credit card. Handing it to the clerk, he said, "I've been told I'm long legged. Is there a full size car available?"

The clerk staring at the credit card, then looking up at Sam, asked, "You Sam Whitehorse?"

Sam, taking his Stetson off and setting it on the counter, answered, "Yes, sir. Is there a problem?"

"No, sir. Just never seen an official tribal Master Card."

"Well we are both here on official business, and we need directions to the Waukegan Police Department. I guess the sheriff is the head law enforcement authority. So how do we get to the sheriff's office?" inquired Sam.

"That's easy. The Lake County sheriff is down on Martin Luther in Waukegan."

After spending over an hour at the sheriff's office, Robert and Sam were directed to the Waukegan Police Department, where after explaining several times to several police officers and finally a person in plain clothes what they wanted to do, Sam was handed a form to fill out requesting a warrant. Filling in all the blanks on the form, the final bit of information asked for was the reason and evidence to request a warrant.

Entering a small office with frosted glass in the door, they spoke to an attractive blonde woman in a nice-looking pantsuit, who said, "You say that two teenage girls and a three-year-old girl are being held against their will by this Al-abadi? No, Mr. Whitehorse."

"It's Sergeant Whitehorse, or just call me Sam," Sam said, leaning slightly forward and looking at her name tag, "Ms. Whitmore."

The attractive Ms. Whitmore replied, "As I was saying, Sergeant Whitehorse, I need something to take to a judge. I don't know how you police on the reservation do it, but here we need at the very least *probable cause* in order for me, or anyone else, to authorize you to go on private property. You bring me something I can use and I will not only get your warrant but I will take my team and go with you."

"Can you at least tell us where this Women's Clinic is?" inquired Robert.

"At the old train station. You go over the train tracks and it is near the lake. There used to be several warehouses and manufacturing plants down there. Now there is a housing development down near the lake. The clinic is located right on Lake Michigan. Before you even think of going there, remember that if you enter that facility without permission you will be arrested."

Traveling down the streets of Waukegan, Robert points towards a gutted-out building. That has to be the old train station. "Sam, I think that's the track that everybody is talking about. Can't even imagine a train running over those tracks. Didn't she say we're supposed to cross the tracks and go down that little hill?"

"Yeah." The sounds of sirens and about four fire engines heading across the tracks drew Sam's attention. "Well, Robert, I do believe that if we follow the circus, we will find the elusive Women's Reproductive Clinic."

The red fire marshal's car and two of the four fire engines blocked the entrance to the clinic. There were people, mostly women, in front of the building.

Robert was the first to notice a dark blue Crown Victoria idling behind them. "Sam, look to your left. Those men standing outside the Crown Vic, isn't that Special Agent Williams?"

"I know my eyes are getting old, but I think you are right."

Looking around, Asa saw houses in all stages of development, from foundation to naked beams and brick and shingle sidings. Lumber, bricks, plumbing supplies strewn over the landscape. The two-story building called the Women's Reproductive Services had tall grass against the side of the building. Behind the building was an old railway spur, where in times past a train may have dropped off a boxcar.

In front of the building there were women. It appeared to Asa that there may have been twenty or thirty women of all sizes, shapes, and colors. Some of the women were obviously pregnant. On the side farthest away from him, near the shoreline of the lake, were children. It reminded Asa of maybe the children in a Day Care Center. They seemed to be of different sizes. *I really need to get glasses. I know there are children, some maybe even teenagers, but at this distance all I see is shape.* "Tom, look over there near the shore line?"

Looking up and in the direction Asa was pointing, "Yeah, so?" answered Tom.

"Doesn't that look like a bunch of kids?"

"Yeah, Asa it does. I need to get closer. That is if I can get past the barricades."

"Asa! Look behind you?"

Wiping his eyes, and turning, "What?" questioned Asa.

"Those two standing back there," Pointing, "that tall Indian. Isn't he a tribal police?" probed Tom.

Motioning for Tom to follow, Asa headed for the two tribal policemen. "Hey, Sam, isn't it?"

Looking away from the crowd, Sam glanced over and then turned to face Asa. "You are the FBI. I didn't know you were involved in this one."

"What do you mean? We're still looking for our little girl, Jackie Gallagher."

Bending down and scuffing his boot on the gravel, "I got a message." Raising his wild eyebrows, "About the little girl, plus there is information that there are two missing teenagers that are here."

The two tribal policemen, and the two special agents started walking to the roped off areas where they spotted children. Agent Tom Walton was about six paces in front of the others. Robert literally skips to catch up with him, "Agent Walton."

Slowing down and turning to face Rides The Horse. he asked, "What is it, officer?"

"Well, Sam and me checked with the sheriff of Lake County. We were sent to the Waukegan Police Station, and after all that, Sam and me were told we could not get a warrant 'cause we didn't have probable cause. So how are we going to look for those kids?"

"Well, Robert—it is Robert, right?"

"Yes. I'm the guy that screwed up by letting someone take that little girl off the Rez."

"Well, Robert, I expect that someone gave you a good talk. And just remember this is the federal government trumps state, county, and city. Plus we do have *probable cause*. We traced an IP address to this very location."

Several uniformed police officers came up to the group of four. "Sorry, you can't go beyond the barricade."

Asa didn't a say a word, he just pulled out his badge, and ID. The police at the barricade lifted the yellow tape.

Walking over to the children and surveying the unusually subdued group of children, they didn't see anyone that they could recognize, but Sam turned to the others, "Have you ever seen a group of kids so quiet? I know they are supposed to be sick, but there is something not quite right about this."

Asa, walking over to the group of kids, turned to face the group of four. "I raised three kids, and even when they were supposed to be sick, it was all my wife and I could do to keep them quiet. I'm not saying that there are times when the illness will knock them out, but there are at least a dozen kids here, and they remind me of zombies."

Bending over with his hands on his knees, between gasp for air, Asa turns to Tom and asked, "What do they have here? The sign says *Women's Reproductive Services*. Are these kids in some kind of Day Care? You know maybe where a mother can leave her kid while she sees a doctor?"

"You all right, Asa?"

After taking a deep breath, Asa answered, "Yeah, just a little winded."

"These kids have been medicated. No five year-old is that spaced." Actually walking in front of each child, and looking, "Asa, I don't see our little girl here. How are Sam and Robert doing?"

Sam, seeing Tom coming over, said, "I don't see our teenagers. We need to get inside that building."

Asa, catching up with Tom, said, "I agree. Hey, boys, looks like we have a welcoming committee," pointing to the large black man, dressed in dark slacks, a turtleneck sweater and a watch cap and a tall skinny blond man in whites. "I don't think they will be very pleased with us," Asa exclaimed, while trying to catch his breath.

Walking up the two white-colored cement steps, and Asa displaying his badge, the large black man seemed to growl, and the blond orderly stepped aside.

Still struggling for breath, Asa motioned for Robert, Sam, and Tom to come close. "Hand me your cell phones."

Tom just handed his to Asa the two Indians glanced at Asa with confusion.

"We don't have hand-held radios, I know we should have." Taking the cell phones of Robert and Sam, scanning and putting his number in the phone. "Now just keep that on speaker; I should be able to talk with you and you with me. I've called our local office, and they are sending backup, but in the meantime we need to tear this place apart before they have a chance to move the girls."

Tom opened double doors and found himself staring at a receptionist behind a counter. Looking directly and the heavyset woman in a nurses uniform, "Why aren't you outside with everyone else?"

Looking up at Asa with a belligerent look on her face, and a very annoying nasal sounding voice, "I knew it was a false alarm. I didn't see smoke or anything and I just haven't got time to waste on these games."

"Okay, just stay where you are, and I mean stay in that chair. You and I are going to have a little talk." Pointing to the metal door behind the receptionist, "What is behind that door?" demanded Asa. Putting his wireless to his mouth, "Can everybody hear me?"

There were three responses. "I need one of you guys up front. I think I need to babysit."

"I've checked most of the offices on the second floor and utility rooms. It seems pretty quiet. I will have to get back up here. Give me two minutes and I'll be there," replied Robert.

Asa was starting to sweat. He moved to one of the stuffed chairs near the receptionist. Putting his hand up to his chest, then digging into his back pocket, pulling out a handkerchief, and wiping his brow.

Just as Robert arrived at the reception, he heard the sound of cars in front. Glancing out the glassed doors, he could see a dark-colored SUV and several dark blue sedans. Looking over at Asa, he commented, "I think the Calvary has arrived." Then staring at Asa, "You're not looking so good. Are you all right?"

Taking a deep breath and then sliding off the chair, Robert came running over Asa, as the receptionist grabbed a sweater that was on the back of her chair and casually walked out the same doors that the agents were entering. Robert ran to his partner and put a finger on Asa's carotid artery, then on his wrist. Looking up just as Sam entered the room, "Sam, Agent Williams is dead."

A uniformed police officer entered followed by FBI special agents. Sam held his hand up and asked, "Are there EMTs out there?"

"Sam! Did you see where the receptionist went? I saw her just before Asa dropped."

The police officer shook his head. "Yes, sir." He turned and opening the doors, he called, "We need EMTs in here."

The EMTs put a sheet over Asa and lifted him onto a gurney, raised the gurney, and wheeled him out.

Special Agent Tom Walton found himself in a large room with an oven in the center. There was a door on the far side of the room. He approached the door and when he opened it his stomach felt as if it dropped. What he saw was a room with at least a dozen teenagers lying in beds on yellow soiled sheets. The girls appeared to be drugged. He heard what sounded like the croak of a frog. Then it sounded like words, "Mister, mister, please."

The girls in the beds all seemed to be unconscious except for one. Tom found the teenager with an IV in her arm. Touching her head, he asked, "What's your name, child?"

Looking up through eyes so swollen that they were barely slits, "Where is Ellen?" she murmured.

"Who are you?" Sam probed.

Barely above a whisper, she said, "I'm Sarah. Where's Ellen?"

Holding her face in his hands, "Sarah, I'll be right back, and I promise we will find Ellen."

Arriving in the reception area, going over to a pale Asa, lying on the floor and scrutinizing the reception area, "Something is wrong," observed Sam and Robert.

Sam walked over to Tom, and putting his hand on Tom's shoulder, said, "Asa is gone."

Looking up at Sam, he asked, "Where did he go? No, he just passed out."

"Tom... Asa is dead."

"How?"

"Pretty sure it was a heart attack."

Several more police officers came to the reception area. "Okay, we need help. I've got a warrant here and we need to go through this building, to looking on every inch," instructed Tom.

"You're right. We need to get back to our search. By the way, has anyone seen this elusive doctor?" remarked Sam.

"Sam, will you come with me? I think I found one of your teenagers, or at least one of them."

Not much bothered Sam. He was able to tolerate many different smells such as rotten vegetation, the carcasses of decaying animals, but the putrid smell of human waste and regurgitation. Perusing young girls, barely in their teens, lying in their own waste. Then he saw her. He pulled a photo of a teenaged girl out of his shirt pocket. "Yes, Tom that is one of the girls I'm looking for."

"Why are you looking so down? You found one of the girls."

"Yeah, but I still need to find the other one, plus the other reason I left Big Sky country. I really thought we would have little Jackie. And of course, your partner. I really didn't know him, but I think he would have been accepted even among *my* people."

"You know, Asa was a Jew, and he used to joke that he was part of the missing tribe of the Israelites. So maybe he really was one of your brothers."

There were women wandering around the entrance when Tom asked one of the police officers, "Tell those women that this clinic is closed."

Several of the women tried pushing past the barricades and the police officers. Tom overheard some say, "What are we supposed to do?" Another said, "Where can we go now?"

* * *

Most of the uniformed men had departed. There were four patrol officers watching the doors. Tom called Sam and Robert to come close. "Robert, did you finish your search?"

"No, Asa called and said he needed help. I checked most of the offices and a couple of broom closets upstairs, but there is a whole area that I haven't looked at yet."

"Okay. Why don't you and Sam finish up together? I'll have the agents from the Chicago office help me with my report. Where is Asa when I need him? He was always so much better at making my reports understandable."

Robert was heading for the stairwell; he turned and looked at Tom. "I know we found Sarah, but we are still missing a teenager and little Jackie."

Sam started to walk with Robert toward the stairwell. "You know I found Sarah and several other women in an open ward just beyond the operating room. I bet there are kids here too."

Stopping in front of one of the agents from the Chicago office, Tom requested, "Arrange for transportation to a hospital for these women. If I'm not mistaken, there will be children to transport. I just don't know how many."

"I need to get back upstairs. I was just about to check the end of the hallway when Asa called. That could be where we will find the little Gallagher girl," declared Robert.

On the second floor, Robert noticed double doors to his right. He opened the doors and found himself in a dining hall. There was a serving area: stainless steel steam table, a commercial oven, and on one side of the oven was a grill and on the other side was a four-burner stove. He saw the walk-in cooler. Opening the door, he saw shelves with wide-mouthed thermos bottles. On the floor was a large stainless tub with potatoes in it. In the back of the walk-in was what looked like a freezer door. Inside the freezer, there were frozen vegetables and large slabs of frozen beef on the shelves.

Coming out of the food service area by a single door in the rear of the kitchen, Robert heard sounds. It sounded like puppies or maybe kittens. He opened the last door in the hallway. What he observed were small beds used as cribs and several toddler beds. There were small children in all cribs, but one in the toddler beds. There were three metal cribs, two had babies in them.

Pulling out his wireless phone, Robert requested, "This is Robert. Can you hear me?"

"Yeah, I hear you. What do you need?"

"I found kids. Small young kids, a couple of babies. I need medical assistance to transport these kids."

"10-4."

* * *

Sam opened a door on the far side of a room that looked like an operating room, with a stainless steel examining table that was probably an operating bed. There was an assortment of scalpels and a pair of scissors on a stainless steel table. He opened the door on the far side of the room. What he saw was the stocky, mousy-haired woman, the same woman that he saw at Crow Agency. She was sitting in an old wooden rocking chair with a fully formed fetus in her lap, with its legs kicking. He couldn't help but stare at the child. It looked as if the child should be crying, except its skull was crushed. There was gray mater puddled around the woman's feet. She had tears running down her cheeks, and she was staring at the wall, rocking back and forth, and moaning.

He finally recovered enough to look around the room. Next to the woman was a shallow ceramic tub. Next to the tub was a deep stainless sink. In the wall were large drawers. The drawers were the kind Sam had seen in the medical examiner's lab. Sam went over to the drawers and started pulling them open.

The first drawer Sam opened had the body of a girl, possibly fifteen years old. She was covered in a blue gown, her black hair was matted against her forehead. She was African American. He pushed the drawer back and opened the drawer near the bottom. For some reason, he knew this was what he would find. He reached in his shirt pocket and pulled out the photo. This was definitely Ellen. The gown she was wearing was bloodied. There was blood that had spread out under her; the blood was now coagulated.

Standing straight and backing away from the drawer, Sam pulled out his wireless phone. "Tom, when the paramedics come, send them back here. You might want to get the medical examiner back here too."

* * *

The sun was glaring through the bedroom blinds as Russell was attempting to pull himself out of bed. His toes and fingers were a grayish blue and felt very cold and painful. His feet were cold and his toes numb, as were his fingers. *How can my feet hurt and feel numb at the same time?*

Trying to yell, but with little luck. Speaking as loud as he could, he said, "Naomi, could you come in here?"

Just then the phone rang. With some effort he did manage to lift the receiver. "Hello."

"Russ, this is Cyrus. I think you might like this."

"Don't keep me in suspense."

"Boy these Feds really take their cyber forensics seriously."

"Get to the point."

"Well at about 0-dark-thirty we finally got a trace on that address."

"Come on, Cy, get to the point."

Sounding exasperated, Cyrus replied. "Sorry, Chief. The FBI team took their Gulf Stream out and headed for Chicago. This may be the news you have been waiting for."

Shaking his hands, then rubbing them together, Russ switched the phone receiver from one ear to the other. "Listen, Cyrus, I'm sorry. I didn't mean to sound like a real son of a bitch. It's just that I woke with the grandmother of all aches."

"I understand. I ain't got kids. I have no idea of what you are going through. I really would like to hear what you guys came up and how you did it."

"Hey, Russ, if you and Naomi are up to it, Sal and I would like to take you guys out to breakfast."

With a sigh, Russ said, "Cyrus, it sounds great, but I don't know where we will find a babysitter in this short notice."

"Just get Naomi and the kids dressed, normal Saturday digs. In other words, out of the PJs. We'll be over in about an hour."

Sitting at a local Denny's, the Gallaghers were drinking coffee with the Grangers while the boys were finishing up their pancakes. Anthony was exceptionally quiet; it was as if he were a thousand miles away. He contributed to the conversations only if someone directed the conversation toward him.

Naomi reached across the table and placed the back of her hand on Anthony's forehead. Looking over at Russ, she said, "He doesn't seem to be running a fever. By the way, how are you doing?"

Closing his hands and making fists, he answered, "Whatever it was, I think it is getting better."

Russell eyeballed Cyrus, "Okay, buddy you were all excited when you called this morning. What did you find out?"

Both women were quiet. Cyrus looked over at Russ. "First, it looks like the little Middle Eastern doctor messed up. He may be smart. The cyber forensic lad is awesome." Russ was looking impatient. "When we left your house the other night we had an idea where your little girls might be, but Doctor Abide was getting greedy. He advertised on the Internet, and according to the cyber guys, he left a fingerprint."

Naomi, with tears welling up in her eyes, implored Cyrus, "Please don't do this. Tell us what you found out."

Rubbing his crew cut, Cyrus was trying not to act too excited. "The good news is…"

Naomi interjected, "Good news! That means that there is bad news."

"As I was saying, Agent Williams and Agent Walton took the FBI gulf Stream as soon as we found out the physical address of the computer that was used to broadcast your baby's picture. They found a facility where they were holding women and children. Tom Walton said that he knows Jackie was there. They rescue a lot of women and children."

Russ looked over at Cyrus, then said, "But not Jackie."

With his face getting red, "No, Russ. Not yet, but it is a matter of time."

Naomi was almost to the point of breaking down. "I'm sorry, Cyrus, but we have been hearing that for weeks now."

"I haven't heard from Asa or Tom since they left. I thought for sure that Agent Williams would at least contact you. They should be checking in. As a matter of fact they should have checked in hours ago. The people at the bureau assured me they would call. Bureau… is that short for bureaucracy, oh that's right. I thought that the air force had their cookie cutters, and dealing in red tape was a military thing."

Naomi and Russell were just staring at Cyrus. Both boys looked first at Cyrus and then their parents.

"Sorry. I didn't mean to start raving. Let me give them a call. Maybe they tried to call."

The expression on Cyrus Granger's face went from a deep red to a very sallow yellow.

"What is it? Did they find our daughter? What's wrong?" implored Russ.

With a breath and a sigh, Cyrus stated, with a catch in his throat, he answered, "The good news is Jackie wasn't there."

"That's the *good* news? What the hell is the *bad* news?"

In a monotone, Cyrus stated, "They are sure she was there, but somehow she slipped out of the facility where they were holding her. There was child in the same room with Jackie. She had been playing like she was asleep when she saw a little boy. It seems this boy was white. She said, not just white but like a white powder, with very pale blue eyes. The little boy pulled the needles out of the little girl's arms and untied her. Evidently he came back and untied that child."

With tears in her eyes, Naomi looked up at Cyrus. "Okay. What about my little girl?"

Cyrus said, "I am only relaying what I heard on the phone just seconds ago. After the alarm went off, one of the agents went into the building, found the room, which just had empty beds. According to Agent Walton, it appeared that Jackie had left the hospital gown on the bed and changed into her clothes. The child that was talking to Agent Walton said that the white boy half carried half dragged the little girl."

Putting his hands behind his neck, Russ commented, "Okay. If that is the good news, what's the bad news?"

"Agent Asa Williams is dead. Tom and the two tribal policemen are searching for Jackie as we speak. Seems they are looking for this little very pale white boy as well," Cyrus said as he looked over at Anthony. Sam, one of the tribal policemen, called the little boy "The Ghost that walks."

Russell stared at his son, then shook his head. Barely audible, he mumbled, "No! That is impossible."

Naomi glanced at Russ. "What did you say?" she asked.

Now rubbing the back of his neck, Russ said, "Sorry. I am having a hard time taking this all in."

Naomi staring at Cyrus, then back down at her coffee, appeared to be getting anxious. "We have to do something. I just can't sit here and wait. It seems like we have been waiting for months."

"Let's go back to the house. We can wait there as well as anyplace else," proposed Russell.

Naomi looked over at Sally. "Why don't you, guys, come over the house?"

Sally looked over at her husband, and then at Russ and Naomi, "We'd like that, but how about we come over a little later this afternoon. There are a few things we need to do." Sally peering at Naomi over her coffee cup, "Naomi I can't know what you're going through. I don't know what to do. We've just met. I'm not sure if I should leave you alone are be with you?"

Denny was just staring at his parents. Anthony seemed to be staring into space.

"I appreciate that, Sally, but I think Russ and I need a little alone time. Plus I don't know what is going on with Anthony. Maybe he didn't get his sleep out. He doesn't seem to be running a fever. Just a little nap should help him."

CHAPTER 19

Leaning against the door frame to what appeared to be a pathology lab, the heavy woman with the mousy hair was still sitting in a rocking chair, rocking back and forth and making moaning sounds. It was obvious to Sam that this woman was strung out on something. Sam had seen and even known people on the Rez that were strung out mostly on alcohol, but he had seen his share of the few that got carried away with peyote, even a few that used pharmaceuticals, but most of them looked skinny, anaemic, sickly, with bleeding gums. He'd seen this woman before.

Darlene was staring into space. She couldn't think of a thing but the scream of the baby as that man squished its skull. *Where is Melvin*, she started thinking, then she felt sounds coming out of her. All she could utter, was, "Melvin… Melvin."

Two large muscular men wearing white arrived at the pathology lab. Sam just pointed to the woman in the rocking chair. One of the men in white looked down into the woman's lap, turned toward the ceramic tub, and threw up. The other man turned to Sam just as Special Agent Tom Walton walked in. "You want her or what?" exclaimed one of the men in white. "Can you take her to the State Mental Health Hospital?" asked Tom.

The man who threw up was still leaning over the ceramic tub. The one by the door replied, "She'll be over at Aurora. I've got some paperwork for you to sign."

When Sam and Tom came back to the reception area, Robert was talking to what appeared to be a girl of twelve, possibly thirteen. Motioning for

Tom, Robert said, "This girl says that she saw the doctor leave with a big man. It looked as if they were in a hurry."

Tom put his hand out to the girl; she backed away. He immediately backed away. "Sorry. What's your name?"

With a shaky voice and sounding as if she were about to cry. "I'm Susann."

"Susann, did you see a little redheaded three-year-old?"

"Yes, sir."

"Do you know where she went?"

"Yes, sir. A little white boy took the needles out of her arms and unfastened the straps that were holding her to the bed. He took her out of the room. I was supposed to be asleep but I was just playing possum. I tried call to him, but my throat hurt and I had trouble yelling. He mist of heard me cause he came back and told me to get the other kids out of there. Then he ran with the little girl. He was half carrying her and half dragging. Told me to hurry."

"Do you know where they went?"

"No, but," pointing to a tall girl with blonde curly hair, "that girl was my babysitter. Her name is Sandy, the white boy got her out too. She told one of the other agents where she saw the doctor go. I don't know what happened to the little girl and the white boy."

Just then one of the agents from the Chicago office came over to Tom. "You have to be Tom Walton from Baton Rouge."

Tom looked up and saw a tall skinny pock-marked man with thick black hair. He said, "You got me."

"I'm Don Wilson, out of Chicago. I hope you don't mind, but when they carried Agent Williams out of here I called it in to the office. I also told the office about what we found here. Told them they would get a written report as soon as I could get to it. I am really sorry about your partner."

"Thanks. I wasn't really thinking about writing reports."

The few uniformed police officer were interviewing the people remaining in or near the Women's Reproductive Services. The children were being gathered by representatives from the Cook County Child Protective Services. Names and addresses of the women remaining were reluctantly supplied by the few women that remained.

Sitting on a pier watching the commotion around a large freighter, Melvin is gazing at the cargo being lifted into the cargo hold. "Larry, what are we doing here? Don't you think we should be putting distance away from that clinic?"

Pacing back and forth, Al-abadi stops and turns to face Melvin. "Relax my friend. We will both be on our way and far from this place as soon as they finish loading that ship."

Running his hands through his thick hair then pulling it back and securing his hair in a ponytail using a thick rubber band, Melvin said, "Larry, we are standing out just sitting here watching a big ship loading cargo."

"You are right, Melvin. Let me find the captain. He knows me and there is a place for us on his ship."

Pushing himself up, "Then what? What happens when we get on board? Where are we going?"

Motioning for Melvin to follow, Al-abadi said, "I see the captain. For you information, we will go through the St. Lawrence Seaway out into the Atlantic. We will be in Damascus shortly."

"Larry, I need to know, what happened to Darlene? She went in to help you and I haven't seen her. Where is she? She may not be much to you, but she has been my woman for a long time."

"Your woman is damaged. She is of no further use to either one of us."

Melvin started to say something just as a dark-bearded man approached. Al-abadi spoke at length, turning to Melvin and motioning for him to follow. "Come we must hurry."

"I will not leave until you tell me what happened to Darlene."

Both Al-abadi and Melvin turned at the sound of cars and sirens at the end of the pier. The man that Al-abadi called captain was at the top of a large gangway motioning for the crane to pull the gangway up.

The small dark Middle Eastern doctor was casually moving toward the dock workers. Melvin looked over toward Al-abadi, just as a uniformed policeman grabbed his arms and cuffed him.

Tom Walton and arrived just in time to see Melvin being placed in a patrol car.

Robert turned to Tom, and questioned, "Is that it? Where is the doctor, the little Arab.?"

"I know you don't want to hear this, but I think he got away by blending in with the dock hands. I bet you've heard this before…"

"Hear what?"

"That they all look alike."

Robert just tightened his jaw and stared at Tom, then with the start of a smile and showing his white teeth, he said, "That is what we say about whites."

* * *

Sitting on a cushioned bench to the right of the reception desk at the Women's Reproductive Services, with his gray, sweat-stained Stetson on his knees, Sam was just cradling his head in his large hands. He heard a sound. It sounded like a young boy's. He felt something tugging at his leg. Looking up, he saw Anthony.

Shaking Sam's leg, Anthony said, with his arm around a very little redheaded girl, "Mr. Whitehorse, would you please take my sister home. I am not sure they are at home. We live in St. Petersburg."

Rubbing his red watery eyes, Sam looked over at Anthony. "Why can't you take her home?"

"I don't know. I tried when I first found her, but couldn't do it."

"Yes, Anthony, I will take your sister home. Will you be there?"

"Yes, Mr. Whitehorse. I will be there. You will like my dad… Mom too."

* * *

Denny was in the backyard. Naomi thought that Anthony needed a nap. There wasn't a sound from the bedroom. Cyrus and Russell were sitting under a shade tree, watching Denny, when the house phone rang. Naomi almost tripped over Sally trying to get to the phone.

Out of breath and dropping the receiver, she said, "Hello, this is Mrs. Gallagher." She dropped the receiver just as Russ came in the kitchen door.

Grabbing Naomi, Russell questioned with concern, "What is it?"

"Russell, Cyrus, Sally—Jackie is coming home."

At the top of his lungs, Russell yelled, "Denny, come in please."

Within seconds, a caravan of a maroon Caprice and a green Jeep Wagoner were heading for the Gandy Bridge and to Tampa International Airport.

Sitting in the Tampa Terminal, Naomi was the first to see Zack Taylor walk the arrival area. With big brown eyes and the look of someone very pleased, he said, "I just got the word."

Pacing back and forth and staring at the arrival board, trying to make the time go by, they were wishing and hoping for the announcement that the flight from Chicago has arrived.

Looking at the tunnel from the tarmac, Naomi remarked, "Someone bought new clothes for our baby."

Jumping out of Sam's large hands, Jackie screamed, "Mommy!"

Holding Jackie in her arms and looking at a large Indian, he said, "You must be Sam. Jack warned me that you would be with her."

Sam looked up at the Gallaghers. "She would need to be examined by a doctor."

Zackery walked up to the group. "Naomi, Russ, it will only take a few minutes, but we have a doctor on stand by."

The End

A SHORT BIOGRAPHY OF
BOBBY BELL

Bobby Bell is a retired air force non-commissioned officer who spent almost thirty years in the military. He started his military career in the United States Navy and spent time in the United States Army, finally finding a home in the air force. Having an opportunity to spend time in three branches of the military and spending three tours of duty in Vietnam, Bobby enjoys telling stories. His essays and articles are published under the pseudonym Raymond Bell.

Bell was born in 1943 in Philadelphia, Pennsylvania. His grandfather was a career soldier. He and his grandparents were assigned to several military installations.

Some of his friends would call him a very good liar. Hs grandmother insisted he was just a good storyteller.

Between serving as a cook in the navy and an air traffic controller in the air force, he attempted to attend a community college with the hopes of learning to write a good story. His counselor at the community college insisted that he would never be a good writer and his writing skills were marginal.

Never one to read books until his time in the navy and his many months at sea, he found himself reading the books in the ship's library and the back of cereal boxes.

With Bell's passion for reading, he found a particular desire to read science fiction. He also did and does enjoy historical novels, literary fiction, police procedural, and mysteries.

As a civilian, Bell worked as a cook and a sous chef in hotels and country club, working his way up to finally managing restaurants. He is presently retired, spending three hours a day as a crossing guard.

Bell is constantly intrigued about the world around him. He recently read an article about human trafficking and had heard stories about people that become addicted and find themselves on the streets selling themselves, normally for sex. Until then, he was not aware that slavery still existed.

Of his many travels, he spent time at the Rosebud Reservation in South Dakota and at St. Joseph's Indian School in Chamberlin. This story is fiction, but the description of the tribal police has been colored by Tony Hillerman, who wrote about the Navajo Tribal Police.

Although this story is fiction, unfortunately, these events take place all too often. In Bell's imagination, it only made sense to have living bodies close to medical facilities where they could be used. Although it is not legal to pay for organs, there are still people who **will** pay a great deal of money for living organs.

Storage and preservation solutions are transported to the donor hospital within the temperature-controlled polyurethane container, and the organs are returned in the same container within an inflatable cushion. This method is the preferred method of transportation of tissue and organs. This method offers advantages over the more conventional methods of organ storage with regard to convenience, temperature control, and sterility.

The science of organ transplants has come a long way. There are many people living today because someone authorized the transplant of a person's organ.